AMYOT

To Cathy

GUY ALLEN

This is a work of fiction. All characters, incidents, and dialogues are products of the author's imagination.

No part of this book may be used or reproduced in any manner whatsoever without written permission of the author.

DRILLING RIG

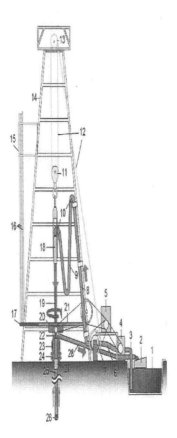

1. Mud Tank
2. Shale Shaker
3. Suction Line
4. Mud Pump
5. Motor
6. Vibrating Hose
7. Draw works
8. Standpipe
9. Kelly hose
10. Goose-neck
11. Traveling block
12. Drill line
13. Crown block
14. Derrick
15. Monkey board
16. Drill pipe (stacked)
17. Pipe rack (floor)
18. Swivel
19. Kelly drive
20. Rotary table
21. Drill floor
22. Bell nipple
23. Blowout Preventer
   (BOP) annular
24. Blowout Preventers
   (BOPs) Pipe Ram &
   Blind Ram
25. Drill string
26. Drill bit
27. Casing head
28. Flow line

Preface to the Second Edition

Amyot was first published as an ebook in 2012. Since that time, on the advice of reviewers, the storyline has been expanded, much of the technical detail has been eliminated, and a Glossary of terms has been included in the Appendix at the end of the book. May you enjoy reading Amyot as much as I enjoyed writing it.

Guy Allen
April 30, 2014

Prologue

The fringes of civilization in Northern Canada are populated with a scattering of small villages. Amyot is not one of them, but in many ways, it represents them all. Why these rural collections of humanity exist where they do can be defined by geographical attractions, a struggling tourist industry, the exploitation of natural resources, transportation routes, or significant historical events. They are peopled in the main by those with the pioneering spirit, who have forsaken the relative comforts of a more southerly existence through economic choice or necessity. Living close to the native peoples has blended and blurred the racial lines over the years. Although these settlements and villages are real, you won't find Amyot on a map. It exists only in the mind of the author.

1

Disregarding the most essential piece of my late father's advice almost cost me my life and will probably haunt me for the rest of my days.

Somewhere off in the distance a bell was ringing. I dragged my mind from total unconsciousness to a halfway irritated state. I rolled over, decided to wait it out, and then go back to sleep, but the noisy creature wouldn't stop. "Damn alarm," I muttered as I swung an arm across the small table by my bed, hoping to grab the clock and end its misery and mine by flinging it into some far corner of the room.

No luck.

All I managed to do was spill half a bottle of tequila, send a couple of books skittering along the floor and knock the telephone into the wastebasket. The ringing stopped. It took a minute for the realization to make its way through the haze that the sound was from the phone, not the alarm. The clock sat innocently all alone, unplugged, as had been the case for the past two months.

I'd had spent a total of sixty-three days of slogging through rain-drenched bush and providing meals for hordes of chewing, biting, and sucking insects, while trying to map a bunch of rocks, which had nothing to recommend them other than the fact they existed. I had been looking forward to a night of blissful sleep after the long thirteen-hour drive from LaRonge. It didn't look like I would be so fortunate.

I lay back with eyes closed and tried to drift away from reality, but I knew any more sleep was impossible. My body was about as awake as it was going to be in its present condition.

"Who the hell would be calling at this time of day," I wondered as I stumbled into my tiny kitchen. One look at the wall clock told me the time of day was just about noon. The appearance of the room was my next shock. It was immaculate with a vase of fresh flowers on the counter, which was bare, instead of being covered with the disgusting messes I usually leave. The dishes were washed and put away, and everything inside the refrigerator was current and recognizable. Even the spaghetti sauce, which had exploded on me before I took off, had been wiped from the walls. Millie had left her mark. Millie Coltron, my guardian angel, owned a small office management business and, as such, handled all my reports, accounting, bill paying and telephone answering. These were the tasks I was either too lazy or stupid to do. Housekeeping was not in our contract, but she kept doing it. This is a double-edged sword, as unsolicited services of any kind from the opposite sex open that little door of warning in my mind, and this was no exception. The specter of possible ulterior motives on Millie's part had occurred to me, but as usual I dismissed

4

any suspicions. Besides, she was a beautiful sweet girl, a good friend, and I hated cleaning up my messes. That little door in my mind was my legacy and sometimes a nemesis, but it had guided me through the treacherous waters of life since adolescence.

When I was young, just into puberty, a wise man provided me with an extensive discourse on his thoughts on life and love. This wasn't the usual birds and bees talk, which is often foisted on budding youngsters. I pretty well had that one figured out through experimentation. This was about life, how it should be lived, and all the responsibilities involved. But mostly he spoke about love, the emotion, and its various forms. He talked of ordinary love, which people feel for parents, children, pets or very close friends. He spoke of why it is so necessary to ease the pain and loneliness we bear. But above all, he talked of romantic love, of how true love was the most important thing in life and was so hard to find and recognize. He spoke of how physical lust is so often wrongly interpreted as love. He saw what he called true love as a very strange fragile condition. When you think you've found it, it slips away in an instant. Many times in your life, he went on, you will believe you are in love, but be wary, and don't mistake something based solely on physical attraction for that very precious condition of a mutually shared genuine affection.

The words were spoken by my father, C. Sheldon Sherant, who was very drunk at the time, as he was on most of the occasions when he felt it necessary to impart these gems of wisdom to his son. He was a man who had found what he had thought was his soul mate. Unfortunately, this attachment only lasted a month, and was not shared by my mother. But Shelly never stopped believing that someday it would rekindle itself, or there was someone else to share his capacity for this precious emotion.

Shelly was an only child: small, shy, and like many single offspring, very lonely. He had been raised in a strict, loveless, uptight Christian home, where rules and punishments were the norms, and hugs and praise were rare. Throughout his early life, he longed for someone to love him, to hold him and to care about him. Then he met the one lady, who in a month washed away most traces of his prior upbringing. So, except for this brief period of unbridled passion, he had experienced little first-hand knowledge of the subject, which continued to captivate him. These limitations, however, did not prevent him from expounding his views to anyone who would listen. His most easily-accessible captive audience was his son. But I did learn a few things, and some of them stuck. After that, my existence consisted of a series of events, which tested Shelly's teachings, prompting me to discard many of them.

"Be careful not to sacrifice yourself for physical gratification. It is fleeting, and the journey can be long and lonely after it's gone. Don't travel my road."

Those words seeped into my subconscious and stayed, especially the part about traveling his road. Shelly's voice located a little room at the back of my mind, slipped in, closed the door, and reappeared on those occasions when I thought I had found my true love. Just once in my life has it failed me.

I did consider Millie to be a close friend, but

with Shelly's years on earth as a guide, I
consistently fought inclinations to take our
relationship to another level.

Although at this point I didn't care who had
phoned, curiosity got the best of me, so I called
Millie's answering service, which was picked up on
the first ring.

"Coltron Office Services, Gloria speaking,"
responded the perky voice.

"Gloria, it's Dusty. Someone rang me this
morning, but I didn't get to it in time. Did you take
it?"

"Mmmm, let me look. No, Millie answered that
one. You want to speak to her?"

"Sure, why not, put her on," I replied, although
I wasn't confident I was mentally sharp enough to
spar with her today.

"Well, you are alive. When I checked in on you
earlier, I wasn't too sure."

"You were here?"

"Who do you think shoveled out your place, the
good fairy?"

"Yeah, I figured you for that act of random
kindness."

"So, you don't remember me taking my clothes
off and crawling into bed with you?"

"Gee, I thought I was dreaming."

"Which is the only way it's going to happen,"
she replied.

"Should I be interested in this phone message?"

"You obviously missed my note. It was Dave
Stenowicz. He called yesterday and said it was
important he meet with you today for lunch.
Today's call amounted to telling me he was at the
Palliser eating his soup, and where the hell were
you?"

"So, you made the appointment for me."

"That's right. I knew you'd be back today, and I foolishly thought you would be sober and conscious."

"You know me better than that. I'd better call him and find out what's going on."

"Hey, before you do, let's get together and go over this last batch of field notes you sent. A lot of it doesn't make sense."

"I figured you might experience problems with my scribbles. Conditions were so bad up there that I tried to cram two weeks' work into a few days. Let's meet tomorrow. Bring that map-drawing gal of yours, and we'll try and wrap it up quickly."

I hung up with the feeling this verbal exchange had ended in a draw.

Dave Stenowicz was one of the golden boys of the oil patch, a gifted geophysicist who had struck out on his own from one of the major petroleum companies after finding them a bunch of gas production in an area of Montana that no one else wanted to drill. We were about the same age, early forties, but he was married with a whole brood of budding scientists. His hatred of physical exercise and taste for high-calorie lunches had slowly increased his lateral dimensions since I had last seen him. Any advice that he should start looking after himself continued to fall on deaf ears.

I had supervised a drill program for Dave a couple of years ago, and we had developed a mutual respect. His ability was well thought of in the industry, but he was not particularly liked. I attributed this to his intensity and single-mindedness, which put a few people off, especially the liquid lunch crowd at the Petroleum Club. We wouldn't be called close friends, but Dave and I got along. His contracts amounted to describing the task or problem and then letting me figure out how to solve it, which is what I like. So, as much as my head and body told me to take a couple of days off before I called him, curiosity again won out.

Dave answered in his usual, lovable sarcastic way.

"So, you didn't die as we all had expected. You do disappoint me, Daryl. That beautiful creature who looks after you tried to assure me you hadn't got my message, but I had vivid images of you passed out in your truck somewhere in the middle of Saskatchewan."

"Gee David; I thought you knew I am immortal."

"Must be a bad connection, was that immortal or immoral?"

Dave Stenowicz hates using nicknames. He insists on being called David and is the only person I know, other than my mother, who calls me by my given name, which is the main reason I don't usually respond to it.

My mother and I sustain what borders on a total lack of interest in each other's welfare. The arrangement works well, as neither of us makes any attempt to establish a relationship. Her treatment of Shelly was our point of departure. On the rare occasions of her stopovers at home, they argued. Instead, I should say, she would make a point of her views, and he listened, occasionally nodding his head. I guess that was one of her joys, making his life miserable during her limited presence. This, of course, set him off on a week-long bender, so that by the fourth or fifth day, I would search out his favorite haunts, drag him home and dry him out. How he was able to keep his job at the University during these times still amazes me. The bonds of tenure are definitely stronger than those of marriage.

Fortunately, I had a more sober mentor. Jeremy Prince and I were good friends from the fifth grade on. His Uncle Fred took us both under his wing. He was Shelly's drinking buddy but was usually able to quit after a couple, whereas father was often the last one to leave the bar. Many an evening I assisted Fred in dragging Shelly home, and he helped me put him to bed. Whenever Jeremy or I needed guidance or directions in getting out of trouble, it was Fred we would turn to. Jeremy's folks were too busy being important people to offer much in the way of parenting.

My mother found her true love at an early age, and it has lasted all her life. She truly cares for herself, and except for that month of abandon with Shelly, which produced me, no one else to my knowledge has ever threatened this narcissistic relationship, though many men have probably tried. Apart from a partial sharing of our gene pool, mother and I retain nothing in common. I've considered this lack of sensitivity on my part as a direct genetic gift from her. Whenever I needed a parent for advice or just some comfort during the bad times, I turned to Fred or Shelly. Mother was always off on another trip to some remote corner of the world in her continuous attempts to teach people of the underdeveloped countries how to live their lives.

Shelly died a few years later, supposedly as a result of his constant consumption of alcohol, but to my mind, he had finally found a release from the life without the love he craved.

His funeral was well attended by his drinking

buddies and co-workers from the University. As usual, as with most events involving our family, his wife was a no show. I checked out on her soon after he passed on.

Dusty came into the world as the result of my supervision of fourteen straight dry holes, or 'dusters,' as they are called, for a bunch of investors back in the sixties, who had them drilled based on some promotional scam. One of the local techie reporters heard about the story, and the name stuck. I would have resented the nickname, but it pissed my mother off so bad when she heard of it, I vowed to keep it.

"I need you to come in ASAP," Dave said with urgency.

"Can't you roll the hoop by me over the phone, and I'll decide if I want to jump through it?"

"No, too sensitive. Does double your daily rate get your attention?"

"For how long, half a day?"

I finally detected a chuckle from Mr. Stoneface.

"More like a minimum of a month but probably three."

"I'll be there by coffee break."

My next task was to transform a denizen of the Saskatchewan bush to a respectable member of the Calgary business community. It was a challenge. I was able to find soap, a razor, and some almost clean clothes.

I located my truck where I had parked it in the underground garage, sitting diagonally across two stalls, neither of which was mine. A couple of nasty notes were stuck under the wipers thanking me, an inconsiderate bastard, for blocking their spaces. I had decided to drive over to Dave's, but after reading these messages, I figured I'd leave the truck where it was, at least for another day.

Stenowicz Oilfield Services occupied the upper level of a converted storefront apartment in what had become a fashionable address in Lower Mount Royal. Dave's wife ran an artsy antique store on the main floor, littered with an abundance of curios, many of which looked to me like things I had helped Shelly haul to the dump thirty years ago. Nevertheless, she was doing a thriving business catering to the local oil-rich clientele. Emily was busy with a customer but responded to my presence with a wave upstairs, indicating Dave was in his office.

"You look like hell," was his greeting.

I nodded, cleared some papers away, and sat down on the only chair not submerged in maps and reports.

"This better be good. I harbor a very limited attention span today."

"Oh, I think it will keep you awake," he replied as he spread out a thick roll of maps.

Geophysical tracings, to the uninitiated, look like the doodlings of a group of drunken chickens. This bunch was no exception. Usually, they show basic information such as location and any critical technical data. However, all I could discern from this assortment was it covered an area somewhere in northeast Saskatchewan, beyond the limits of places, which most sane people would visit by choice.

"What am I looking at, David?"

"Before I explain it to you, I need you to sign this paper certifying that you will not disclose anything you learn about this project to anyone."

"Don't worry; in my present condition, I'll not

remember much of what you tell me anyway. How about I verbally assure you? I try to avoid signing papers like that. It helps lawyers justify their existence when someone screws up."

"I know, but one of the backers made it a condition for putting up the money."

"Okay," I replied as I signed the form. The whole thing was beginning to make me uneasy. I had gut feelings telling me to walk away. Dave put some weights on the top map and proceeded to explain.

"As you no doubt guessed by the coordinates, this covers a thousand square mile block of ground north of the town of Meadow Lake. I've heard it's not the most desirable country to be in during the winter. Did you ever work there?"

"Yes. I just came out of that part of the world but to the northeast of your area. Meadow Lake is not a bad town, and there are other settlements up there, Ile a La Crosse, Amyot, and some tribal villages. This is a mixed population: whites, Métis, and Crees. It's not particularly desirable to visit at any time of the year."

"Well, you may be going there again. As you probably know, my oldest son James is taking geophysics at UBC and working as an intern with a bunch of engineers in Vancouver. They had him doing a lot of interpretation work from government and private aeromagnetic publications. You've seen these maps, where they fly over an area with an instrument that measures the magnetism of the ground below. Last summer, he was helping me clean out all the old files and reports, which had collected over the years when he came across old magnetic charts of this part of Saskatchewan. They are primitive technology, but he pointed out several

13

interesting unexplained areas with magnetic patterns that show a form of closure. He did some research on them, but there is very little available data. These circular anomalies of high magnetism may represent local spots where small buried hills of granite exist beyond the Precambrian Shield, which has been mapped to the east. If that is the case, the younger sedimentary rocks would be deposited along the flanks and on top of these bodies. If some of these sediments were porous and contained oil and gas, and if they were overlain by tight dense rocks acting as traps, then we could be sitting on productive reservoirs of hydrocarbons."

"That's quite a bunch of 'ifs, David, but I can imagine where it might be possible, and as you know, a lot of holes have been drilled on much weaker arguments."

"I know. I've been involved in some of them."

"So, how do you support your theory?"

"Well, first of all, we ran magnetic surveys using instruments on the ground to verify the information on the airborne maps. That negated some of the closures but identified others, which didn't show up on the aeromagnetics. Over these spots, we ran some other surface surveys to substantiate the data. We defined about a dozen small closures randomly spaced throughout the block. We believe they are buried granite structures but with limited areal extent. Some of them, however, could be small pinnacle reefs in the overlying limestone strata, although those types of rocks are rare in this area. We believe our ground surveys define the contact zones between the steep sides of these circular bodies and the surrounding rocks. Our hope is that the sediments are porous and capped. There could be some oil or gas pools. We have no record of small reservoirs of this nature in the area, but gas is produced to the west of our block, and those wells show good production records."

"A couple of things strike me. Haven't any of these ground surveys been run over this area before? Also, I would think there must be some old drill records of holes up there from sometime in the past."

"There is, but the drilling has been focused more toward the Alberta border, looking for gas pools or extensions of the tar sands. The surveys are old, wide-spaced, and with one exception, miss our prospect areas."

"So, what's the deal?"

"We plan to drill test holes on three of the most promising structures, and we want you to look after the project. These are extremely 'tight' holes. We can't afford any information leaks, as the whole program is time-sensitive. We have the key areas tied up, and the rest of the block has been posted for a land sale during the first part of January. We are initially planning the three holes and possibly six to follow, but we want to see the initial program completed and all that data processed before the sale bids are opened. A Mid-Continent rig has been contracted at a bonus rate to do the drilling. The first two holes are on land we have already put under lease. The location for the third well is set, and we are presently negotiating a deal with the owner. The contractor's key people are signed to secrecy, and we told them to handpick their crew and camp personnel. We are arranging for a secure communication system to the outside world."

"So, when do you want me up there?"

"We're pushing a road into the first site now,

and the rig will follow in about a week. They should be set up and ready to drill in ten days. Can you make it by then?"

"I guess I must make an effort if I don't want them to start without me. You did say double my normal rate. That makes it six hundred a day and expenses."

"I am aware of your rates, and there's one other thing. A group of environmentalists is urging the Federal Government to set aside much of this area as a National Park, similar to Wood Buffalo. They've got the natives all fired up, convincing them that they'll pull in some cash from the tourist trade. This could be a problem. We don't know how organized or militant this bunch is, however, it's something to be aware of."

"That's not logical, David. There's nothing up there to protect, except a few moose that are well adapted to look after themselves."

"I know, but it doesn't have to make sense if the Government buys into it."

2

After the long drive, too much alcohol, and limited sleep, things were moving too fast. I knew I needed to take some time off, but the adrenalin had kicked in and masked my fatigue. I also knew I had been drinking too much, and it was beginning to bother me. Even Millie was starting to make snide little remarks about being surprised to find me sober after a job. As I get older, the hangovers are requiring more time and effort for recovery. But most of all, I was concerned I was traveling down another of Shelly's bad roads.

What I needed now, along with ten hours of uninterrupted sleep, was food and a meeting with Marty Kallock. For the present, I opted for the last two. I phoned Marty, and he arranged for us to meet at a trendy little bistro on Eleventh Avenue. This was the current hot spot for the after-work crowd and Marty's favorite hangout. It didn't open until just before lunch and was usually still going strong in the early morning hours. The place was all glass and glitter and continual selections of current music that steadily increased in volume as the day and evening progressed. Marty and I had held meetings there a few times before. I was never sure whether he favored the place because it was close to his office, or he just wanted to have a good seat to review the evening's crop of lovelies. By the time I arrived, he was on his second coffee and absorbed in a serious conversation with a teenage waitress less than half his age, who was hanging on his every word. It was three-thirty, the quiet time between the lunch and the dinner crowds, so we pretty much had the place to ourselves. Marty is my age but looks at least ten years younger. He is tall, lean, with broad, muscular shoulders tapering down to a waist size most office workers would envy. He still has all his hair, a thick brown wavy mass that laps neatly on his collar. Always impeccably dressed, he seldom allows himself to be seen in a suit unless the corporate world demands his presence. It is immediately apparent, especially to the ladies, that he works out regularly at the gym when he is not trekking through the bush in some God-forsaken corner of the globe. He runs his own exploration contracting service specializing in looking for mineral deposits anywhere in the world. As he describes it, his work consists of long periods of boredom punctuated by the occasional adrenalin rush of a valuable discovery. I have worked for him and with him several times over the last few years. He is a friend and one of the few people in this business whom I trust and respect for his abilities in the bush. For the past two months, I had been working for him, running a satellite camp to map and prospect some mining claim blocks in the Foster Lakes country of northern Saskatchewan. He ran the main camp at the north end of Lac LaRonge. The arrangement worked well as I could send my progress reports to him with the pilots on the supply flights that serviced both our camps. He had closed the big camp a couple of weeks before I pulled out, and I knew he was anxious to be brought up to date on the results of my work.

I eased into the booth across from him and ordered a coffee, steak sandwich and a piece of pie from the young waitress, who barely acknowledged my presence, she was so intent on soaking up Marty's line.

Finally, when she managed to pull herself away, he said, "I called your service, but the girl told me she didn't know where you were. I got the impression she wasn't too sure where she was either. Surely that wasn't this great business manager you've been telling me about."

"No, that was Gloria, the receptionist, and you're right, I often have the feeling she's not dealing from a full deck, but hey, she's great to look at and knows which end of the phone into which to speak. However, even if she does know where I am, she's paid to say that. It drives my creditors crazy."

Marty has a short attention span, and I sensed I was losing his, so I went on.

"I guess you're wondering what I've been doing the past few weeks for all the money you haven't paid me yet. Well, I've got some of the stuff here in rough form to go over with you. Millie says she can have the final maps and reports to you in a week. Does that work, or are your clients hounding you for it?"

"No more than usual," he replied. "They're pretty happy with the program so far, but we need to talk about a couple of other things before we get started. Did the Mounties fly into your camp?"

"Not while I was there, but they may have

come while I was out in the bush. Rollie never said anything about it, so they probably didn't, or he would have told me. Why?" The grave look on Marty's usually smiling face was beginning to unnerve me.

"They are investigating the disappearance of a couple of prospectors. It seems these fellows were landed up in your neck of the woods before you got there. LaRonge Aviation dropped them off, and they haven't been seen since."

"Where were they dropped off?"

"Northeast end of Lower Foster. You know that spot just below where the water runs down from Middle Foster. There's an old campsite on a ledge that sticks out into the lake."

"Okay, I know where you mean. I used that spot a couple of years ago."

"The cops told me the story of what they knew, which wasn't much. They said they checked all through the camp and found nothing to give them any idea what had happened. There were some tent poles cut, a food cache built, and some burnt rocks from a fire pit but no food. I got the impression they had no idea what they were looking for. They evidently just flew in, described what they saw, and flew out again."

"No tent, canoe, or tools?"

"Nothing. They figured it was strange these fellows started to set up camp and then just left. By the way, did Reuben show up at your camp? When we were finished, I sent him up there to help you just before we pulled out. He was happy to go, as he didn't want to return to town. He had his canoe and some gear and set out cross country."

"He showed up but never said you sent him and sure wasn't much help. He just sat around and ate and kept pestering Rollie to go fishing. Being his son-in-law, Rollie was kind of torn as to what to do. They caught a lot of fish, but at that stage, I didn't care if they fished all day; I just wanted to get the job done with as little hassle as possible and get out of there."

"Well, I don't think I'll be hiring either one again. Reuben used to be a good worker, reliable and sober, but once he got a few bucks and got into the booze, he started going downhill."

"You know that was the second time Reuben was up in the Foster Lake country. He was there with Rollie building camp when I first flew in. I was surprised to see him, as I thought he was with your crew."

"What?"

"Didn't you send him up there?"

"No, we shut down for a week about then. Reuben said he wanted to go into LaRonge to stay with his daughter and was insistent on knowing when we were going back into camp so that he could get a ride, but he didn't fly with us back to town and never showed up to return to camp. I remember thinking it was kind of strange at the time."

"That is odd. He didn't mention you had broken camp. He just up and left a couple of days after I flew in. By the way, what were the names of those two prospectors who went missing?"

"Just a minute, I've got them here in my notebook." After thumbing through a few pages, he replied, "Lucien Veneau and Gerard Richard."

With the mention of the names, something familiar clicked in my head, but I couldn't quite tie it down.

"Marty, do you know these two?"

21

"No, I had never heard the names before the Mounties gave them to me. I don't think they are locals. That was another thing giving the cops trouble. They'd had no luck in backgrounding either one. No one they asked around LaRonge or any of the settlements had ever heard of them."

Then it hit me. When I was about a week into my survey work, I had found two claim posts with tags and very little line blazed. I was almost sure one of the names scratched on a tag was Veneau. I relayed this to Marty.

"Did you copy down the other stuff on the post: claim number, dates, and such?" Marty asked.

"I'm pretty sure I did, but I need to check my field notes. Let me call Millie and see if she can find it."

I put in the call and got a hold of Millie just as she was leaving the office. She was on her way home, but since she would be passing near our meeting place, she offered to drop them off.

"Just bring all the August notes; that way, I'll be sure to have what I need."

Millie arrived half an hour later. She is one of a select few ladies who can shut down conversation when they enter a room. My back was to the door, but I knew the exact moment she came into the restaurant. Marty's eyes went glassy, and his jaw sagged. He never did finish his sentence. He just stared past me. Marty is notorious as a real smoothie with the ladies and endeavors always to keep this reputation intact. In spite of a surprisingly stable marriage, his romantic conquests are legend. I had not seen him speechless until tonight. Millie sauntered over and sat down next to him.

"Hi, I'm Millie, you must be Marty," she announced.

Marty was stuck for a reply.

Millie handed me the field notes, and as she started to leave, said, "Dusty, I hope you two have more luck translating this stuff than I did."

At that point, the waitress finally showed up with my sandwich.

"Can you stick around for a few minutes and go through them with Marty? This is the first thing I've had to eat today, and I'm starving."

Marty had suddenly found his voice and was all charm, inviting her to stay for dinner with us, but she politely declined, indicating she was on her way home to prepare a meal for her son. She did agree to stay long enough to decipher my strange abbreviated note-taking methods for him. After she had gone, Marty quizzed me about her until I had to hold up my hand to stop him.

"Yes, she is very beautiful and sweet, and smart, and no, we are not into a relationship. She is my friend. She's a widow with a twelve-year-old son, and as far as I know, she is not hooked up with anyone, but you are, and I would not like to see you hurt her."

"Sounds like you are more interested in her than you admit."

I thought about it for a minute then answered, "Maybe, but I don't want to screw up a good arrangement by getting serious with her. I find her very attractive, but my life is too unpredictable and complicated to hook up with anyone right now or in the foreseeable future."

Meanwhile, leafing through my notes, Marty found the reference to the claim posts.

"Here it is," he announced, "IP for CBS 5638, staked August 2, 1985, by L. Veneau. You indicate there was a metal tag, and the blazes ran southerly for about fifty yards and then nothing. Did you go down that line any farther to see if there was a final post?"

I remembered making those observations and thinking it was odd at the time there was no direction to the final post indicated. The blazing stopped suddenly a short distance from the initial post.

"No, I figured it for inexperienced stakers. I didn't bother following the line to check for another post."

"How come you were southwest of Jenny Lake?" Marty asked. "Our ground is to the east."

"Yeah, it was by chance. I was looking for an easier way to get around that big muskeg area south of the lake."

"I know what you're saying. I tried the same thing this spring when I was in there. There's no way you can avoid it. The date on the post is interesting. It was put in on the second. We sent Rollie in to build a camp around the seventh or eighth, and you arrived on the fifteenth."

"That's right, and Rollie said that Reuben had been there a few days when he arrived."

Marty rubbed his forehead and stared past me. "That means Reuben may well have been in there at the same time as the stakers and might have had contact with them. The timeline makes sense. He didn't show up to start with us until just before you went up there. I think I need to pass this on to the cops in Prince Albert. They need to talk to Rollie, and especially Reuben."

The remainder of our discussion centered on the results from my final days in the field. The reconnaissance prospecting and mapping program had been moderately successful. In all, I had located: a small silver-gold vein with visible gold, a substantial radioactive area, which my scintillometer indicated as a thorium/uranium source, and a low-grade disseminated copper-molybdenum showing of indeterminable extent in the granite. All were interesting and needed further investigation. Now, Marty's concern was to convince his clients that these results warranted more work for them to loosen their purse strings and commit to a detailed exploration program. We parted with my assurance to him that I would have the final maps and reports on his desk within the week.

3

The dawn of the next day brought a remarkable improvement to my disposition and physical condition. I felt I had rejoined the human race on a trial basis and was almost normal. Early to bed for the first time in weeks, and sleeping well into the morning did wonders. By noon I was showered, shaved, and attired in clothes, which had not spent the last two months with me in the bush. I was as mentally ready as I would ever be to struggle through the translation of my field scribbles with Millie. I strolled through the slush across the bridge over the Bow River to the yuppie area of Kensington, where Millie had her office above an art gallery, which was doomed to bankruptcy. She was waiting for them to fold so that she could expand to both floors.

Today she was dressed in what I referred to as her 'power outfit,' a beautifully tailored dark blue suit with all the accessories matching perfectly. She usually looked good. Today she looked great.

"You really shouldn't have dressed up for me today," I announced as I entered her office. "I'm getting quite used to you looking frumpy whenever we get together."

"You wish! Truth is I have a meeting later with a potential client who should prove to be able to pay on time and potentially be much less of a pain than you."

Two other girls, Gloria, the vacuous receptionist, and a typist, occupied the outer office. In Millie's private room, Mapgirl was slumped down in an overstuffed comfortable chair in the corner. Mapgirl's name was Karen, or Sharon or Erin. I was never sure. I suspected she changed it each time we met to confuse me. She was a third-year Geography student at the Calgary campus with an artist's flair for creating masterpiece maps from the rawest of data. Her personality was almost non-existent, bordering on obnoxious, but her talent was incredible. She was a desperately thin haggard girl with straggly grayish-brown hair that roamed across her face when she moved her head. Her complexion was a dull gray, pitted mess. She was one of the few females I have encountered who would not necessarily look better if she was cleaned up. Her wardrobe, a product of the Salvation Army Thrift Store, consisted of a large bulky sweater of indeterminate age and a pair of man's combat pants. She was a radical contrast to the immaculately attired Millie.

"Well, Mapgirl, what have you got for us so far?" My intention to piss her off was not a smart thing to do, but the tendency to push people's buttons is one of my many character flaws. Some people just have that effect on me. I have to find their buttons and press them. I had noticed that she did much better work when she was angry, which was generally most of the time.

"My name is Faron, and I wish you would use

it when you speak to me."

"Damn, you've changed your name again. I hope it has had some effect on your social skills."

"My name has always been Faron. You're just too stupid to get it right," she screamed.

I felt maybe I had gone too far in goading her this time. Millie wasn't helping the situation much, sitting there with a smirk on her face. She did, however, motion me to back off.

"Here are the maps. This was all I could translate from that mess you call field notes. If you could learn to write in a language we both understand, it would help."

I had a perfect retort, but this time I held my tongue. The maps were beautiful, an absolute perfect interpretation of the area I had examined. I realized I needed to make amends with this strange girl.

"Faron, these are excellent. You did an outstanding job."

She was speechless, and for probably the first time, I detected a smile.

It was Millie's turn.

"Here is the rest of the report. I received all the assay results and inserted them in the Appendix and also keyed them to the report and maps. I left your photographs out. Dusty, you need to take a course on how to use a camera. Everything is out of focus except your thumb. I've included five copies, three for Marty, one for you, and I'll keep one here in the office for when you screw up, lose your copy and come crying to me. I think that wraps it up except for paying us."

"Which I'll do right now," I said as I dug out my chequebook.

I bundled up Marty's copies, tucked them

under my arm, and headed downstairs. I heard
Faron clumping along behind me. She caught up
with me at the front door, grabbed my arm and said,
"Why do you try to hurt me whenever we meet?"

She tried to keep her composure but couldn't
prevent a single tear sliding down her cheek. I
realized my usual lack of sensitivity had prevented
me from seeing the vulnerability of this girl through
her tough veneer.

"Faron, I'm truly sorry. I don't want to hurt
you. I guess it's just sort of my way."

We were standing outside a coffee shop, so I
suggested we go in, sit down and talk. For some
reason, I felt it was necessary to let this poor girl
know someone was interested in her as a person.
Our conversation was superficial. I asked her about
her likes, her dislikes, her plans for the future, and
anything I thought a young woman would like to
talk about. It had the desired effect. She became
animated and began to smile more often. The only
area where my interest was noticeably not welcome
was in her past. I became quickly aware she was
unwilling to answer these questions. When we
parted, I believed it was as friends.

I sent Marty's maps and reports over to his
office by courier. He phoned later in the afternoon
to announce his client was more than pleased with
the results.

"By the way," he added, "I called the Mounties
in Prince Albert and told them what you said about
Reuben being up in the Foster Lakes country about
the time those guys disappeared. It seems they knew
about it. Rollie told them, but they haven't been
able to find Reuben. Evidently Rollie came back
into LaRonge alone."

"That's right. I had Rollie flown home a couple

of days before I left. Reuben took off in his canoe the next morning. Is he is still out in the bush?"

"Nobody knows where he is; even his daughter claims she hasn't heard from him."

Millie called around four to invite me to dinner, an occasional event, which continues to confuse me and jar loose a warning from Shelly's ghost.

"Tony's been asking me when you can take him fishing again. Maybe you could set something up before you leave."

"Sure," I replied hesitantly. "What time do you want me to come over?"

"We have dinner at about six. Does that work for you?"

"I'll see you at six."

Tony Coltron, Millie's son, was a mature twelve. Usually, I don't like to be around kids. All their bad traits remind me of what I was like at their age, and I didn't much like myself then. At least this kid had a mother who cared about him.

After Shelly was buried, my mother finally showed up three weeks later. Her first task was a brief, perfunctory visit to the gravesite. Next was her problem of what to do about her strange son.

"I have decided to keep the house. After all, the housing market is depressed, and you need a home. You have two choices. I can enroll you in a private boarding school, or you can live here on your own and stay in the local high school. I won't be around much, but I'll arrange for someone to come in once a week to clean the place. If this is your choice, you have to stay out of trouble, or I make some other arrangements. It's up to you."

I chose the second option. Even with Shelly around, I had primarily been on my own, and the prospect of boarding school was, in fact, no option at all. I wasn't about to enter a life of others telling me how to live after years of being only accountable to Shelly when he was sober. The arrangement was the envy of many of my high school friends who lived under sets of rules imposed by their parents. Most of them longed for my total freedom to do what I wanted when I wanted. They didn't realize I somewhat envied their stable home environment and families that cared and supported them. If asked to make a choice, I would probably still have opted for my situation. It could have been disastrous as I was usually game to try anything, but fortunately, I was smart enough to recognize the line between adventure and danger. That part of the game, Shelly, had taught me well. His nagging little voice in my brain helped me avoid many relationship disasters and situations of potential danger, and Fred Prince was always around to help me sort out the tough stuff.

Tony was a good kid. Millie had done a great job as a single mom while being a successful career woman. Her husband, Tony senior, had been killed in an auto accident ten years previous, and because his blood alcohol level was fractionally above the legal limit, the insurance company had weaseled out of paying on his policy. Millie didn't receive a cent. I was dating her sister Barbara at the time, and she asked me to find a good lawyer so that Millie could fight for the insurance money. I wasn't much help, as all the lawyers I knew at that time were either crooked, stupid, or both. The one she did find was hopeless, cost her two grand, and lost the case. My relationship with Barbara ended soon after when she realized she preferred girls and food to men.

Millie had come a long way in the decade.
Tony had grown a few inches since I had seen
him last and had passed the line from boy to young
man. His voice was deeper, and he had inherited the
good looks of both parents.

"Hey, Dusty," he greeted me. "I was wondering
when you were coming over again."

"You know I won't let my fishing partner
down."

"Yeah, like when can we go?"

"We'll figure something out before I leave
town. How about Saturday?"

"Sure, that would be great."

"Okay, we'll take the canoe and get your Mom
to drop us off near Cochrane and float down the
Bow to Edworthy Park. There should be a few fish
waiting for us out there."

Dinner was great. She served my favorites:
baked spareribs with mashed potatoes, gravy, and
lemon pie. Talk centered around Tony and his
frantic approach to the teenage years.

After he disappeared to his room, Millie poured
us some coffee and settled down next to me on the
sofa.

"I didn't say anything before, but I'm
concerned about this next job you're doing. I don't
think you should take it."

"Why?"

"I don't know exactly, just a feeling I have. I'm
bothered by all the hush, hush about it, and the fact
that Stenowicz is the force behind it."

"It's funny, that was my first reaction when he
laid it all out, especially the part about signing the
confidentiality agreement, but what have you got
against Dave?"

"Well, the buzz on the street is that he's not

someone you want to do business with. He has the reputation of getting involved in a lot of needless lawsuits of his own making. One of my clients just got through settling some petty little difference with him on the interpretation of a contract. He didn't have a good word to say about Stenowicz's ethics or honesty."

"Look, Millie, I know he's not popular, but he's a lot smarter than some of those bozos who put him down. I've never had any problems with the work I've done for him in the past, and he's always paid in full and on time, which is more than I can say for most of the promoters in this town."

"Did you know he was having an affair with his secretary?"

"No. I wondered where she was when I went up to see him."

"Emily caught them and told him to choose who was going to leave, her or the babe."

"That shouldn't have any bearing on this job."

"Okay, but don't say I didn't warn you if something bad goes down."

By now, Millie was sitting very close to me, to the point that the little door was easing open, and Shelly's voice was coming through. Tonight she was especially attractive in a simple print dress, which accentuated all her curves. Combined with a subtle scent, which must have been loaded with pheromones, she was almost irresistible. I wanted to hold her in my arms and let nature take its course, but Shelly's advice kept echoing in my head like a broken record. I got up, refilled my coffee cup, and sat back down a little farther away.

"Do I frighten you?"

"Sometimes, you scare the hell out of me, but this is something else. I am lousy at relationships, as you know. You are my friend, probably one of my best friends, and I do care for you. I don't want to screw this friendship up by taking it to another plane and things not working out. You deserve much more than I have to offer."

"I know that. I was checking to see if the ground rules have changed."

"I wish I could say they have, but with my lifestyle, it wouldn't work."

"You could modify your lifestyle a bit. I heard Imperial offered you a job looking after their wildcat drilling operations."

"Where did you hear that?"

"I ran into Jeremy downtown about a week ago, and he told me they had mailed you an offer."

"Yeah, I thanked them but told them I wasn't interested."

"Why? From the way Jeremy described it, it sounded like a good deal."

"It probably would be for most people, but it is mainly an office job, and that is not an option as far as I'm concerned."

"Well, maybe someday you'll want to be with me bad enough to change your style."

"Maybe."

I went back to my apartment that evening with mixed feelings. The whole scenario was like a scene from a movie of my life, which had repeated itself many times during my high school and university years with different female leads. I felt I was living in a loop. At first, I would be strongly attracted to someone who would seem out of reach, but when a relationship began developing on its own, I would start mentally backing away, using Shelly's advice as a cover for my fear. I kept hearing Shelly's voice in my head congratulating me on my unemotional handling of this relationship. I had escaped being tied down again, but on the other hand, I may have started on the road to losing her completely.

Saturday was a typical Alberta fall day: cool, crisp, and clear. Not a cloud was to be seen. It was a great day for a trip down the river. I dug my old freighter canoe out of storage, rounded up the life jackets, paddles, and fishing gear, and headed over to Millie's. She took my truck and dropped us off at a small picnic site by the river, just south of the town of Cochrane. With all the proper warnings to her son not to get wet or forget to eat and all the other mother stuff, she left with my instructions as to when and where to pick us up later in the day.

"Better get baited up and cinch your life jacket before we get started," I said as we carried the canoe down to the beach.

"You're beginning to sound like Mom."

We launched the old canoe from a shallow backwater dug into the beach and climbed in. After his first wet episode, I had taught Tony how to get in by carefully placing his feet along the centerline of the canoe to prevent tipping. We made a leisurely run through the upper part of the river, which was relatively straight with only a few gentle meanders. The day had warmed up, and we saw a few people along the banks fishing or just catching the last bunch of rays before winter set in. It was one of those days when even the effort expended in trying to catch a fish seemed like a task to be left for another time.

Tony was stretched out in the bow with his head on the spare life jacket and was starting to doze off when suddenly the rod jumped in his hands, and the line went tight. Immediately he was wide-awake and quickly loosened the drag on the reel to let out more line. I back-paddled, trying to move the canoe upstream or at least keep it steady in the current.

"Dusty, I think I'm snagged on something, and it won't pull loose."

I had by now paddled out of the main channel and was holding the canoe steady, but Tony was still losing line.

"Looks like your snag is swimming upstream. You're almost out of line. You better cut it and let it go," I hollered.

Determination was written all over his face, and he tightened his grip with both hands on the rod. He was not going to let whatever it was get away. The line went slack, and I was convinced the fish had freed itself. However, at that moment, another major surge took rod, reel, and boy over the side and upset the canoe, launching both of us into the main channel where the current was the fastest. The boat took off like a shot and almost immediately disappeared around the next bend. Tony was bobbing along temporarily supported by his life jacket, which, unfortunately, he had neglected to buckle on securely. At least he had his on. I had been using mine as a cushion, and it was long gone.

"Let go of the rod and swim to shore," I yelled as I floated along behind him, but by now we had moved into a wider part of the river, and he was too far ahead to hear me. I swan as hard as I could downstream, but I couldn't catch him. I could still see him ahead of me, but as I reached the bend, I lost sight of him and began to panic. I swam across to the opposite shore and ran along the bank, but he was nowhere in sight.

Ahead of me was a large poplar, which had

been uprooted where the bank was undercut. It was down with its dead branches spread halfway across the river. The current had stripped away the leaves, and I was able to catch a glimpse of orange in the branches. Tony was tangled in there, lying face down in the water. I jumped in: pulled him loose, dragged him up on the bank, laid him out, and began to apply pressure to his chest rhythmically. The minute or two before he responded seemed like hours, but finally, with a lot of coughing and throwing up, he came around. He was soaking wet and shivering uncontrollably.

"I've got to get him warm and dry," I thought, as I looked around for fire material. There was a plentiful supply of dry grass and small branches, and fortunately, my small waterproof pack of matches was still in my pocket. I managed to get a good blaze going in minutes.

I pulled Tony in as close to the fire as I could without singeing him. Gradually his shivering subsided. I peeled off his wet clothes and laid them over a makeshift frame of branches on the other side of the fire to dry.

"What happened?" He croaked. "Where's the canoe?"

I explained what took place, and he seemed to understand but was still dazed by the ordeal.

"What's going on down there?"

The voice came from the fence line at the top of the bank. An older gentleman in work clothes was leaning on the other side of the fence, looking down on us. As soon as he figured out what was happening, he scrambled down the bank. He had a slender build and moved effortlessly to us.

"We had an accident on the river," I replied. "I'm trying to get the boy warm and dry. He almost drowned."

He took one look at Tony and said, "I think we'd better get him up to the house. He doesn't look so good. Here, wrap him in my coat and carry him. You need to head along the bank a short way to the trail that leads up to my place. I'll put out the fire and follow you."

I did as he directed and found the easy trail up to the modest farmhouse. I knocked on the door, which was answered by a rush of warmth and a short, plump gray-haired woman. The old gentleman was right behind me, coming up the walk.

"This is my wife, Martha. I'm Gerald," he announced.

Martha took control of Tony, leading him to a big comfortable chair in front of their fireplace, where a steady blaze was giving off enough heat to warm the room. He was still shivering.

"We've got to get him into something warm; he's freezing," she said. "We have some of our grandson's old clothes here. Something should fit him. Gerald, go dig around in that drawer upstairs and see what you can find."

"I need to make a phone call from here if I could," I said.

"Of course," Martha replied. "It's through there in the kitchen."

This was going to be a tough call, telling a kid's mother he almost drowned. Millie's response was mostly what I expected, fright bordering on panic. I tried unsuccessfully to calm her down but told her she needed to drive down here and get us. Since I had no idea where we were, I had to call Martha to the phone to give her directions.

"Your wife seems pretty upset," Martha

announced after she had hung up.

"Yes, she is upset, and no, she isn't my wife. Tony is her son. I'm just a friend of the family."

"Oh," was her brief reply.

Millie must have broken every speed limit in the Province getting there. She rushed through the door without knocking and grabbed Tony. She thanked Martha and Gerald profusely and rushed her boy into the car. I also thanked the folks and assured them I would return the clothes. She was sitting there, revving the motor as I climbed into the back seat. She was angry. I wasn't sure if it was at the situation or me.

It was a silent ride back to town. Her jaw was set, and she was looking straight ahead as she sped down the highway. I attempted to tell her the story, but my mental antenna told me she was seething and that just about anything I said would set her off. We pulled up in front of their house, and I quickly got out and headed for my truck without saying a word.

"Dusty, wait!" Tony called. He ran up and gave me a big hug. "I'm sorry about losing the canoe. Maybe we can go look for it."

"Don't worry about it. Canoes are replaceable. You are not. I'm just glad you're okay."

By that time, Millie was in my face.

"He's not okay. He was scared and almost died, and just because you had to put him into danger with this stupid canoe trip. It's obvious I made a big mistake in trusting his care to you. Well, don't worry, it won't happen again."

By the end of her tirade, I was as furious as she was, but before I could reply, Tony cut in.

"It's not Dusty's fault, Mom. I stood up in the canoe and dumped us. He saved my life."

With that, he walked into the house. Before Millie could say anything else, I climbed into my truck and drove home.

4

All day Sunday, I pondered the events of the previous day, but there was a lot of preparation to take care of, so I busied myself getting all my wellsite gear in order and packed for the trip north. I knew it wasn't my fault, so I sure as hell wasn't going to apologize or try to make amends. If she ever came to the conclusion it was merely an accident; we could talk about it. Until then, I had more important things to do.

Because of the remote locations of these wells, I packed a backup radio transceiver and antenna. I had heard the mobile phone reception existed in that area but was very spotty and dependent on weather conditions. Experience had taught me that the times you were most in need of the service were the times it was most likely to be unavailable. In the afternoon, I tuned and serviced my Landrover. Even at twenty years old, it was still the most reliable vehicle I knew for these conditions.

Then I went for a long walk along Memorial Drive. The beautiful autumn colors that graced other more moderate parts of the country were scarce in Calgary. Cottonwoods lined the pathway. During the summer, they showered all who ventured into their realm with a snowy sprinkling of pollen. But now, in late October, their branches were stripped of all foliage and formed a skeletal network over the walkway. As I hiked along the well-worn path, I caught myself paying particular attention to the riverbanks on the chance the canoe might have gotten hung up and hidden by some of the clusters of brush, which lined the shore. By dusk, I realized I had wandered far from home and had a long walk back. At least it gave me time to resolve the Millie situation. I was still angry at her reaction but to some extent, understood it. I was glad I hadn't voiced my feelings in the heat of the moment. I still needed our business relationship.

At home, I got cleaned up, and by midnight I had caught up on my correspondence and reading and was drifting off to sleep when there was a knock at the door. I had no idea who would be calling on me at that time of night, but I stumbled into my clothes and opened it to a very drunk, half-naked Faron.

"Can I come in, I'm frozen?"

My first reaction was to say 'no,' shut the door and go back to bed. She was the last thing I wanted to deal with, but curiosity and the compassion I had developed for this wretched girl got the upper hand. She was barefoot and shivering uncontrollably. Only a wet, old army coat partially covered her tiny frame. Her hair was a mess, hanging over her face and streaked with mud. Tears had spread makeup around like a bad road map. As she stumbled into the room she slipped, and the coat tumbled from her naked body. I caught her before she hit the floor. She clung to me in desperation, shaking violently as

I carried her to the sofa and covered her with a couple of blankets. She tried to talk but was shaking so hard no words would come out. I filled the bathtub with water as hot as I could stand, carried her into the room, and lowered her gently into the tub. It took half an hour before the shivering abated, and she became coherent. In the meantime, I had brewed some coffee and tried unsuccessfully to get her to drink.

Then haltingly, the story came out. A classmate had invited her to a party about a block from my place. She didn't know most of the people, but there was a lot to drink and all kinds of pretty little pills to try. She had passed out because the next thing she knew, she was lying on a bed without her clothes, and her friend was on top of her. From that point, she seemed confused, but the gist of it was, she got away from the boy, couldn't find her clothes, grabbed the first thing she saw to wear and ran out into the street. She knew where I lived, as she had come to my place one time with Millie when I was away. She decided that she would be safe here.

"I feel sick," she moaned as she climbed out of the tub just in time to throw up into the toilet. After a session of tossing everything, she stretched out on the bathroom tiles. She was too weak to get up, so I carried her back to the sofa, put one of my shirts and a pair of sweats on her and wrapped her again in the blankets.

"You need something to eat. I'm going down to the Seven Eleven and get some food."

"Please don't leave me," she pleaded. "I don't want to be alone. I want to stay here with you tonight."

I assured her I would be back in a few minutes

and left for the twenty-four-hour convenience store. When I returned, the sofa was empty. She was lying naked on my bed again, fully awake.

"I am so alone. Will you hold me and make love to me?" She asked, reaching out with her thin arms.

I looked down at her frail naked body and felt no sexual attraction, only pity. I didn't answer, but took her by the hand, led her into the kitchen, put the sandwich and a cup of tea in front of her and urged her to eat. Now that she had sobered up and was warm, I was starting to get fed up playing nursemaid.

"Where do you live? I need to take you home."

"No! I want to stay here. Please let me stay."

I was too tired to argue. I told her to take my bed, and we would sort it out in the morning.

I didn't bother to undress but curled up on the sofa. I must have fallen asleep immediately. The next thing I heard was Faron in the bathroom, vomiting, and crying uncontrollably. The shakes were back, and she was burning with fever.

"This is past my limit," I thought, and in forty minutes, I had her bundled into some clothes and driven to Emergency at the Calgary General. Fortunately, it was a slow night, so the attendants had her on a gurney and whisked away in a matter of minutes. One of them pointed me to a cubicle and said, "You need to register her over there."

The registration desk was under the control of a very large matronly woman. Her short-cropped pixie haircut framed a fleshy oval face, which I suspected was not the harbor of many smiles.

"You brought that young lady in. We need these forms completed before we can treat her."

"I'm not going to be much help. I don't know

her very well."

"Name?"

"Whose, hers or mine?"

"Hers, unless you want us to find a bed for you too."

"Faron."

"Is that a first or last name?"

"First, I think, but as I said, I hardly know her."

"Can you put us in touch with someone who does?"

I gave her Millie's name and phone number and went home.

My head had no sooner hit the pillow than the phone rang; at least it seemed that way. Daylight streaming in the window was the first clue that I had taken more than a short nap. Memories of the previous night flooded into my consciousness, and I knew it was Millie before I picked up the receiver.

"Faron's dead."

"What?"

"She died around seven this morning. I was with her. I think I'd better come over; we have to talk. I need to know what happened before the police get to you."

Millie arrived about half an hour before the police showed up. There was a noticeable improvement in her mood, but at this point, I didn't care. My mind was still having trouble processing last night's crisis and Faron's resulting death. I had just completed recounting the events to Millie when I had to go through the whole drill again with the cops. The pair, a male and a female, were less than cordial, and I had the feeling they were debating whether to hold me as a suspect as part of the cause of Faron's demise.

"Why did she come to your place?" The lady

cop asked. "Did you two have some relationship?"

"Not that I was aware of. I got the message she was at a party nearby and left in a hurry. This was the nearest place she knew to get help."

"So, she has been here before."

Millie answered that one, explaining that Faron had been with her on a visit to my place.

The two seemed satisfied with our answers, which was good, as I was getting a little tired of their attitude and questions.

"Just don't leave the city until we find out what happened," her male counterpart finally contributed as they left.

"Then you'd better solve this quick. I've got a job up north to go to next week."

"You certainly weren't very obliging," Millie observed. "You seem to be pissing everybody off these days."

"That's probably true, but I haven't had a lot of sleep, and those two had an irritating effect on me the minute they walked through the door."

"Yeah," she replied, "It's sort of like the effect you have on a lot of people."

There didn't seem to be any point in launching into a discussion of the trip on the river, so when I finally got rid of Millie, I went back to bed for the rest of the morning.

Monday brought me back to the reality of my next job. I called Dave and set up a meeting for the afternoon.

"Who is doing the drilling?" I asked.

"Mid-Continent. I thought I told you."

"You probably did, but I wasn't retaining much information at our last meeting. That's a good choice. Do you think you can get their operations manager, Stan Michaelson, over to the meeting?"

"I'll try," Dave replied.

Ten minutes later, he called back, informing me they would send their operations vice president, Larry Kirsten, in his stead.

"David," I replied. "That idiot Kirsten is too stupid even to find his way to your office. We need to have Michaelson or whoever is pushing the rig. Do you know who that will be?"

"Umm, some fellow named Slawski."

"Okay, I've worked with Lonesome Luke Slawski. He's a good man, a bit strange, but knows his job and runs a clean, efficient rig. Somehow we need to get the message across that Kirsten has to stay out of the picture and not show up on the lease."

"I hear you, but I don't know how you're going to pull that off. How did he get that management position if he's such a screw-up?"

"His old man owns a big piece of Mid-Continent," I replied.

Thankfully the meeting was held in Mid-Continent's boardroom. Getting four people into Dave's office would have been equivalent to fitting the Calgary football team into a Volkswagen. Another plus was the absence of Larry Kirsten.

Stan Michaelson was an oilpatch veteran, having worked his way up through the ranks from roughneck to operations manager of a major drilling company. He was a big man, probably six-four and nudging three hundred pounds. His few strands of gray hair crossed in some sort of a weird comb-over from both sides of his head. His face was fleshy with the flush of a serious drinker. Most of the muscles of his younger days had gone soft and south. He was, however, still a commanding presence and not someone you would want to take on in a barroom fight.

Luke Slawski was as obscure as Stan was imposing. Both men were in their sixties; however, Luke lacked the ambition and personality to move up the corporate ladder. He was slim and wiry and very tough. Ten years previous, I had been witness to him taking on two of his roughnecks and thoroughly whipping them. He was a man of few words, hence the 'lonesome' nickname, but I liked the guy. He was reliable, knew what he was doing, and respected others that operated in the same manner. We had done a couple of tough sour gas holes together, and both went down without a hitch.

Dave started things off.

"We have all had a good look at the drill plan and should have an idea of what to expect. The program is for an initial three holes with the possibility of additional locations depending on the first holes and the land sale results. These first holes need to be drilled and tested by no later than the end of January. That works out to a hole per month. If the first two are completed before Christmas, we can turn the crews loose for the holidays. But most important, these first two are to be super tight holes. All employees need to sign non-disclosure forms and realize they will stay in camp at least until Christmas. By then, the bid deadline will be passed, and we can loosen things up a bit. Are there any questions?"

I turned to Stan, "What's the situation with the road and the drilling rig?"

"The road's done and in pretty good shape, and the rig is moving out of town today. We should be starting up in about a week."

"We've got the crew together. They're on their way in," Luke drawled.

"Who have you got for drillers?" I asked him.

"Mostly the same ones as the last hole we were on: Big Tom, Dozey, and a new fellow you probably don't know, Vince Cabolchuk."

"What about Danny? He was drilling on that last hole."

"Oh," he sighed. "Danny messed up again, missed a couple of shifts, and got a girl pregnant. The problem was her father was the local Reeve and just about run us out of the County. I've got Danny working derrick on this job."

"Have you heard anything more from these environmental folks who want to shut things down up there?" Dave asked.

"No," Stan replied. "Evidently there is a couple from a militant group trying to stir up the natives to protest us moving in there, but so far they haven't had much luck. The folks on the reserves realize any type of development in the area means jobs, and they sure as hell need jobs. I don't anticipate any problems, but you never know what some of these people are capable of."

After the meeting, Dave and I went back to his office to work out the final details. He seemed a bit nervous as we went over the geology of the prospect again.

"David, what's bugging you?"

"Well, there's one other thing. You know Martin Angleton, don't you? He owns a big brokerage house back east."

"Don't know him, but I've heard the name."

"Well, Martin put up a big share of the money in this project. He has a kid, Kellie, who just graduated from SAIT in petroleum technology and needs a job. One of the conditions for Martin's investment was that the kid could go out on these wells and learn wellsite operations and all the tasks involved from you."

"You have to be out of your mind. You know I work solo, and I am not a teacher, mentor, tutor, or nurse. The last thing I need up there is some adolescent screw-up following me around all day asking me what I'm doing. Can't you find another playground for this juvenile?"

"Daryl, I would if I could, but Angleton asked specifically for you, and this whole deal would not have gotten off the ground without his money."

"Why me?" I had buried my initial concerns about the job, but now they were resurfacing.

"I guess your fame precedes you," he replied.

"Yeah! Sure. Look, I'll give it a shot, but if the kid's a total disaster, we explain it to Angleton and close the school. While we're at it, what other surprises do you have, which you haven't told me about?"

"That's it. If the kid doesn't work out, I'll take care of it," Dave agreed.

Somehow, I wasn't convinced.

5

Time was running out. I planned to leave by the weekend but still had a bunch of loose ends to tie up. I figured the trip would take two days to get to the wellsite if the weather cooperated. The police had gotten in touch and informed me I was free to leave town, but they needed a point of contact in case they had further questions about Faron.

Millie called the following day in her business mode. I was waiting for her to decide to talk about the canoe trip, but it wasn't mentioned. I brought here up to date on the project and how we had to set up communications and data transmission. We decided on standard procedures with a bit more secrecy. Regular daily reports would be by mobile telephone with sensitive information conveyed over land lines. When necessary, we would use a simple code we had developed. After finishing with the arrangements, she announced, "Faron will be cremated the day after tomorrow; the police released her body this morning."

"What did they find out about her?"

"Not much. This is so strange; she doesn't seem to have a history. They couldn't locate any records of birth, parents, schools or anything. She set up a fake identity somewhere down the line. I didn't bother to get references for the work she did for me since she was only part-time."

"Didn't the University check her out when she applied? How did she get in?"

"She went in on an adult admission program, passed the entrance qualifying exams, and they let her in."

"But she was only a kid."

"No, Dusty, she gave her age as thirty-something."

That stopped me until I thought about it.

"What about the bash she claimed she escaped from? Did the cops check it out?"

"They found the place down the street from you, as she said. It belongs to a friend of one of her classmates. They talked to the people who were at the party. They all agreed she had brought the pills and wolfed them down with booze. Of course, she's not around to deny. They probably cooked up the scenario before the cops talked to them."

"What about the cremation? Are you paying for it?"

"Well, the cops haven't located any relatives, so I thought I would cover it since nobody else has offered."

"How about I split the cost with you?"

"Sure. Thank you."

That evening, as I was getting ready for bed, Marty called.

"Hey, did I wake you up?"

"No, but in another few minutes, you would have. What's happening?"

"Got a call from one of my contacts up in LaRonge. He went down to the Mining Recorders Office to check out some claim maps and found some new claim blocks staked up west of Jenny Lake, about half a mile from our ground. I asked him to go back in this afternoon and find out the name and address of the owner and the staking date. He called me back this evening. They were staked a week ago and registered to Mary Sabreau."

"That's Rollie's wife."

"And Reuben's daughter," he added. "I'll tell the Mounties in Prince Albert in the morning."

"No sign of Reuben yet? Is anybody looking for him?"

"Not that I know of."

I hit the road early Saturday morning. The trip involved fourteen hours of driving, definitely a long day. It meant I would be trying to find a drilling rig, which might not be up and lighted, in the dark. I'd been down that road several times before and felt I was getting too old for any more of those midnight searches. Instead, I figured with reasonable weather and road conditions, the trip to Meadow Lake would be an easy drive and would give me light the following day to find the lease road and the rig. The radio forecasted an Arctic cold front moving in within the next day or two. Hopefully, I would be set up on the lease with some heat in my trailer by then.

I took Highway 2 north, bypassed Edmonton, and cut over to 55 at Grand Centre. The road was mostly bare with only a few patches of black ice. Beyond, on 55 through North Battleford, conditions steadily deteriorated to a packed plowed road to Meadow Lake. Fatigue from fighting the blowing snow convinced me my original plan to stop for the night and do the final run the next day made sense.

The next morning was sunny and cold. Fortunately, some enterprising road crew had been up before dawn and plowed the road north. I drove into Amyot around lunchtime. With a population of a couple of hundred regulars, the village has been overlooked by most of the travel brochures. During the summer and fall, a bit of prosperity comes with the influx of a hardier breed of fishermen ready to take on the numerous varieties of biting and stinging insects to sample some excellent northern pike fishing in the local lakes. Somehow the tourist publications for the area have omitted noting the presence of world-class mosquitoes. The main street of Amyot is three blocks long. At some time in the past, blacktop covered the full length. The road ends at the focal point of the village, the hotel, a two-story frame structure with peeling paint, and the apparent presence of wood rot, which forces one to step gingerly to the front entrance. The building dates back to the forties when the village and surrounding area had a few more people. Clustered along the street are the usual businesses: a bank, drugstore, hardware, coffee shop and a general merchant, which provide the essentials for locals and those passing through. A combined post office and police station complete the list. As with most northern settlements, the hotel bar is the meeting place of the village, although a social center and a two-sheet natural-ice curling rink had since been built. Immediately north of the town was a Husky truck stop, where I stopped for lunch before taking off into the bush.

The lease road joined the highway two miles to the north and wound its way for close to ten miles through the seemingly endless stands of spruce and pine. Deep furrows with lots of potholes had evolved as a result of moving the rig and other heavy equipment into the drill site.

I drove onto the wellsite at dusk and was encouraged to see the rig up and running. My shack was the usual ATCO wellsite trailer with living quarters at either end for the geologist and engineer, separated by a double bathroom. I was doing the geology but sharing most of the engineering duties with Luke Slawski. Nonetheless, I was surprised to see his truck plugged into the other end since, usually, the toolpusher has his separate living accommodations. I hauled my stuff out of the truck, got set up and then went to see him.

"We spudded in this morning and should be running surface casing tonight. I had the boys measure the pipe and figure out the hole depth for you. The cement truck is supposedly on its way," he announced as we settled in. "Some guy from the service company came in and set up your gas detector yesterday."

"Anything special I should know about this one?" I asked.

"Well, it's one of Mid-Continents newer rigs, and most of the crews are experienced. Got a couple of young local lads who are as dumb as stumps, but I'll keep them on lease cleanup. So, it should go okay."

"What about the camp?" I asked.

He hesitated. "I'm a bit concerned. Big George Makovic is running it and doing the cooking."

"I know Big George from a job a few years back. He ran a good camp then."

"I know, that's not what's bothering me. He's got his kid Ellie working as his assistant. She's about sixteen and very attractive. Danny knows her and tells me she is somewhat promiscuous; only he uses more colorful words. Coming from Danny, that is disturbing news. I had a talk with George, and he committed to keeping a tight rein on her, so we'll see. Is there anything special you need?"

"Just sample catchers who can find their way to the shale shaker without a map. Do you want me to run orders to the drillers through you?" I asked.

"No, we've both been doing this long enough to know what works. Just post them in the doghouse, and if there are any problems, I'll get back to you."

The first week went without a hitch. We drilled out the cement plug in twenty-four hours and made fast hole through the upper beds. Our good fortune came to an end on Friday when Luke informed me that one of the roughnecks had gotten into an argument with his driller, tossed a wrench down the hole and walked off the job. They needed to fish it out with a magnet before they could go back to drilling. At least, it was a chance to get caught up on some sleep.

A knock on the trailer door brought me back to reality. It was Danny.

"Time to get up," he announced. "I figured after a week of this crap you'd be ready to go to town and get drunk."

It seemed like I'd just dozed off, but the darkness told me I'd slept away half the day. I invited him in, although I was a bit reticent about committing to a night of revelry, as partying with Danny Saponi was not for the fainthearted. He had survived a fifteen-year checkered career in the oilpatch, working his way up from roughnecking to pushing his own rig before he was twenty-five. But good fortune, along with hot women and booze, had taken its toll, and now he bounced around between drilling jobs. As a result of his most recent misadventure, he had been demoted to working derrick. He was in his late thirties but looked like he had just gotten out of high school. With his tall, lean, muscular frame and curly black hair, he was still a lady-killer.

"You go ahead," I said. "I'll catch up. I've still got a few things to do."

"Okay, I'll see you at the bar."

Before I headed for the village, I wrote a summary report for Dave and a brief note to Millie to be put in the mail.

The weather had warmed up a bit after the last storm, and even this late in the day, the thermometer seemed to be stuck in the low twenties. The sky was clear, and the moon's brightness almost made headlights unnecessary.

The barroom at the Amyot hotel was a carbon copy of most of the bars in rural Canada, although this one was a bit older and dingier than most. A stand-up counter ran along one wall for the full length of the room. Two bartenders were kept running, pouring beer and highballs for a room full of thirsty patrons. The clientele covered the full racial range of whites, Métis, and Cree. At the back were three old pool tables, which were in continual use. Tables and chairs were arranged haphazardly around a postage-size dance floor, filled with a gyrating mass of humanity, presumably moving to the sound of a three-piece band, which could barely be heard over the noise. Smoke and the smell of sweaty bodies hung in the air. I looked around for Danny and finally spotted him talking to a young native woman at the end of the bar. I started walking toward him when someone yelled, "Hey! Here's the big rich oilman from the city. You gonna buy us all some beer, rich oilman?"

Suddenly the noise died down, and I noticed

several people staring at me. I paid no attention and
kept walking to where Danny was sitting. He was
looking at me and pointing to my right. Just as I
glanced over, the voice bellowed out again, "Yeah,
you asshole. I'm talking to you. Get your fat wallet
out and buy the beer. Whadda you waitin for?"

By now, the whole room was quiet. The band
had stopped playing, and everyone seemed to be
looking my way. The man behind the voice was
sitting at a table beside the now empty dance floor.
He was huge. Even seated, I could tell he was well
over six feet tall and close to three hundred pounds.
A head of long stringy red hair and a dirty red beard
framed his flushed face. As he got up and slowly
walked toward me, I saw he was more muscle than
fat.

"Maybe I'll have to take that wallet away from
you," he growled.

Experience had taught me that dialogue or
diplomacy was not going to defuse this one. I took
my wallet from my pocket and held it out for him.
Just as he went to grab it, I flipped it to Danny and
kicked the big man in the groin in one motion.
Surprisingly, he didn't go down. He just stood there
a bit stunned for a moment, but then the fire came
into his eyes. I backed up and unfortunately got
caught between two tables as he came toward me
again. One of the tables was empty, but two women
and a man occupied the other. The big man closed
in blocking my way out and moving quickly. Out of
the corner of my eye, I saw one of the women stick
her foot out and trip him. As he fell forward, I
braced my hands down on the two tables and
brought my foot up, catching him on the point of
the chin with the steel toe of my boot. You could
hear the bone crack across the room as he crashed to

the floor. This time he didn't get up. I leaned back against the wall, took some deep breaths, and tried to calm down. As I started to walk away, the man at the table beside me got up and walked toward me. He was about five-eight, with a slight build and a bit of a gut. He looked to be about my age and was dressed in the usual cowboy fashion.

"This one I'm ready for," I thought, getting set for the next attack, but he was smiling and had his hand extended.

"We've been wondering when somebody was going to face up to Moose when he's drunk."

I shook his hand, and he continued, "He's okay when he's sober, but a few beers make him mean. Why don't you join us? I'm sure you could use a good strong drink after that."

"Yes, I need a drink, or maybe two, but someone should look after him. I think his jaw may be broken."

We were looking down at Moose, who was still stretched out on the floor but whose moaning and groaning indicated he was starting to come around.

"It's okay. That's his wife and her brother coming over to get him. I'll see if they are able to take him to the doctor."

He pointed toward a plump native woman with a younger man in tow. We all helped them get the big man on his feet and out the door to their truck.

Back inside, the man introduced himself, "I'm Barty, Barty Stacker, and this is my wife, Anna Lea."

He nodded toward a slim, tired-looking young woman with washed-out blonde hair. She affected a smile, touched my hand, then quickly drew away and reached for her beer. She had a fragile beauty, but I was immediately struck by the sadness in her eyes.

"This other lovely lady is Elena. She lives next to us and teaches at the local school."

Elena's smile was as warm as Anna Lea's was distant. She was young, mid-twenties, I guessed, with an open friendliness, which immediately got my attention. Her long jet-black hair and olive skin were accentuated by a simple white dress that hugged the gentle curves of her body. She was beautiful.

"Why did you stick your foot out to trip him?"

"I don't know. It just sort of happened. It seemed like the thing to do."

"Well, thank you. If it wasn't for that move, he would have had me. I am forever in your debt."

"Hmmm, and how do I collect?" She bantered with a smile.

As the evening progressed, I could sense a connection evolving with this beautiful girl. I made polite conversation with Barty, and Anna Lea about his job, their family, and life in Amyot, but my concentration was on Elena. When the Stacker's left for a series of line dances, we zoned in on each other.

"You live with Anna Lea and Barty?"

"Not exactly, I rent the trailer they used to live in before they got the house. So, it's separate but on their lot. They gave me a good deal on the rent, and it's warm and comfortable. I was lucky as there isn't much in the way of decent accommodation to rent around here."

Further dialogue revealed this was her first teaching job after graduation. She was from Edmonton, and what was of greater interest to me, she was single without a current boyfriend.

She seemed genuinely interested in my work

and my strange background.

The crowd started to thin out as midnight approached. Danny had long gone, dropping my wallet off as he ushered his new friend out the door.

"We should be heading home," Barty announced. "I've got an early shift at the gas plant tomorrow. Are you ready to go, Elena?"

"You go ahead," she replied. "I'll get a ride with Dusty."

I hadn't offered, but all of a sudden, it seemed like a great idea.

Barty hesitated, obviously concerned for her welfare.

I assured him I would deliver her home safely.

We stayed until closing, lost in our new world of learning as much as possible about each other in the time left. It all flowed so naturally, with no verbal contests or games or concerns about saying the wrong thing. It was exciting. It felt like she was the girl I had been looking for in all those destructive relationships of my younger years.

"When will you be in town again?" She asked as we pulled up by her trailer.

"I never know. It depends on what's going on with the well. If you'd like, I'll call you if I get a break, and maybe we could have dinner together."

"I'd like that. If you can get free next Saturday, I want to invite you to take me to the dance at the Community Center."

I was lost in thoughts of Elena as I drove back to the wellsite. About eight miles from town, a large pine had fallen across the road, blocking any further progress. It seemed strange, as it hadn't been there when I drove out. As far as I knew, there had been no heavy winds to uproot it. I expected to see the root clump at the bottom, but the tree had been

GUY ALLEN

cleanly sawed off near the base. Attached to the trunk was a crudely lettered sign, 'Drill in your own back yard, not ours.' Fortunately, I had my chain saw in the back and was able to cut a log out of the center and push it out of the way with my truck. Another mile down the road, a group of medium size spruce had been dropped in the same manner. Another hour was used up clearing them out of my way. This time the sign announced, 'Get out of our sacred land. This is a warning'. Just before I reached the lease turnoff, I came across three large rocks in the center of the road. This time the sign simply said, 'Get Out'. By now I was getting thoroughly pissed off with the whole routine. The rocks were too large for me to physically roll off the road, but using the truck I was able to nudge them far enough to get through.

When I finally got on site, I woke Luke up to see if he had any idea what was going on. I had torn the signs off and gave them to him.

"Beats me," he said. "You and Danny have been the only traffic on the road all day, and as far as I know, Danny hasn't made it back to camp yet. It sure looks like this bunch of environmentalists are trying to get under our skin. We need to keep alert. These folks are not known to give up easily."

6

For the next few days, Elena was continually on my mind. "You're acting like a school kid with his first crush," I kept telling myself, but she had crawled into my head and wouldn't let go. What was more surprising was that my thoughts about her had not allowed my little mind-door to open, nor had Shelly's advice seeped into my consciousness. Initially I put my attraction down to the souring of my relationship with Millie. It seems I have always needed a desirable female to play a lead role in my fantasies.

Tuesday, in the middle of the night, which is usually the case, the gas detector alarm in my shack went off, waking me from another erotic Elena dream. By the time I pulled on my clothes and climbed up to the doghouse, Dozey had stopped drilling and was circulating the drilling mud, waiting on my orders.

"Got drilling break, so I thought I'd tell you. About to send someone to get you up," he said as I opened the door. "You musta had a good gas kick to get you over here so fast."

I nodded agreement and asked how big a break it was.

"Drill time from eight minutes a foot down to two. I cut five feet and then stopped drilling."

"Any gas bubbling in the mud?"

"Couldn't see any."

"Well, keep circulating until I have a look at the drill cuttings."

The samples showed clean, white quartz sandstone with excellent porosity, but unfortunately, no oil stain. It was a tough call, whether to test or just keep drilling, but since they had to pull out soon to change the bit, I decided it was worth a drillstem test to determine if the sandstone held gas or salt water. The tester assured me he would be on site in three hours to set up. Since a trip out of the hole would take up two, I told Dozey to keep circulating the drilling fluid for an hour then pull out. With nothing more to do, I went back to bed. The tester's truck was an hour late.

"I had to push a bunch of rocks off the road to get through. It looks like someone doesn't want you to have visitors," he announced as he handed me two more warning signs.

We ran in with the test string just as the sun peeked over the horizon. The mercury had dropped about twenty degrees during the night, and it was cold. A quick glance at the thermometer showed twenty-five below, which sent me back inside for warmer clothes. The boys on the rig floor stomped around, trying to keep warm as the tester hooked up his pipes and gauges.

"Let's crank her up," he called to Dozey, who rotated the pipe to open the test tool. A small amount of gas bubbled into the pail within a minute, followed by a continuous flow of salt water.

One of the worst jobs for rig hands is pulling a string of pipe full of salt water in subzero temperatures. Usually, it won't freeze unless the temperature is really low. It can't be pumped into the mud tanks because of contamination, so the roughnecks have to unscrew the pipe joints and try to get out of the way as the water pours out over the rig floor. Their anger is sometimes directed at the person responsible for calling the test. I figured it was as good a time as any to spend the rest of the day somewhere else.

I called the school when I got to town, but Elena couldn't get free until four.

My next call to Dave Stenowicz left me puzzled. Contrary to previous conversations with him, I sensed apathy on his part about our progress. I put it down to disappointment in the test results and let it go at that, but it did leave me with an uneasy feeling.

Next came Millie. I went over the progress report and a list of items I needed sent up.

"Is anything wrong?" She asked. "You sound strange like you don't want to talk to me. Are things going badly?"

"No, just the usual screw-ups and lack of sleep."

That seemed like a strange observation from her after the events on the river. Only then did it hit me that I no longer had any interest in our personal relationship or our verbal sparring. I ended our conversation with the distinct feeling I had handled it poorly.

Millie informed me that Marty had called and wanted to talk, so I put a call into him.

"Good to hear you are still alive up there," Marty answered on the first ring. "I thought I'd better bring you up to speed on developments in LaRonge. I got a call from the Mounties. Someone found what they figure is Reuben's canoe and camp gear up by the Mission but no sign of him. It was the same scenario as the prospectors who disappeared by Lower Foster. The camp was only half set up."

"What was he doing way up there?" I wondered. "The Mission is a long way from those claims."

"Yeah, I know, I figure he might have been on his way over to that settlement on the Narrows. His brother lives there. And get this! Rollie's been down to Regina trying to shop some claims to a couple of the exploration companies there. A friend of mine who looked at them told me he's got some pretty good looking gold and copper samples. I don't know if the Mounties are going to contact you or not. Millie says that she hasn't heard anything from them."

"What kind of canoe did they find?"

"I hear you. Reuben's canoe is distinctive. You'd think they would have mentioned that. By the way, what did you do to that beautiful girlfriend of yours? She did not mention you in a loving way."

"It's complicated, Marty. I'll fill you in over a beer next time we get together."

I thanked Marty and hung up. The whole thing didn't make sense. Everything suggested Rollie should be the target of suspicion, but I couldn't buy it. I thought I knew Rollie well enough to reject any ideas of him being involved in something like this. He just wasn't that bright or dangerous, but something about the whole sequence of events bothered me, like a missing piece of a puzzle. I just couldn't drag it into my consciousness.

I picked Elena up when school let out. The school building dates back to the 1940s, when it housed all eight grades in one room, with one teacher for all. Now, with a modest increase in the population and additions over the years, eight grades were divided into four rooms with four teachers. Elena had grades three and four. The room had the usual collection of crayon art, framed motivational advice, and pictures of exotic places from around the world, which most of these kids would never visit.

Watching her from the doorway scurrying around gathering odds and ends and straightening desks, she still took my breath away. Form-fitting sweater and skirt in matching shades of blue accentuated the curves of her body. Even with little or no makeup, she was amazingly beautiful.

"Hi, you're right on time," she cheerily acknowledged my presence. "It must be nice to have all this spare time to come and visit."

"Well, you know, I don't shoot pool, and it's too early to go to the bar, so not much else to do but come see the prettiest girl in town."

"Do you want to go curling?"

"Curling? What, do you want me to do, your hair?"

"No, you know what it is. A bunch of us find a sheet of ice and throw rocks at each other."

"That is a good description, and one of the reasons I've been very careful to avoid it."

"Well, not today. The four of us here at the school have a team, which is part of a curling league. We play the folks from the bank tonight. One of our guys is home sick, so I volunteered you to take his place. We meet down at the rink in about half an hour."

"But, I've never curled in my life," I replied.

"You've spent all this time in Alberta, and

you've never curled. I don't believe it."

"That's right. I've led a very sheltered existence."

"Come on," she urged. "We'll have fun."

We arrived at the rink just as the flurries that had welcomed the day matured into a full-fledged snowstorm. Elena had nestled beside me on the ride over, and I could still feel the pressure and warmth of her body as she got out of the truck.

"I need to phone the rig and see what's happening. I'll catch up with you."

I called Luke and explained that I would be delayed in getting back.

"Take your time, Dusty," he replied. "I'll call the rink if we need you."

I thanked him and was about to hang up when he continued, "And, by the way, we have a surprise for you when you get back."

I stared at the phone, wondering what the hell could possibly be a surprise out there.

The curling rink was an old, unheated wooden shed, just big enough for two sheets of natural ice and a small area at one end for people to sit on a bunch of folding chairs. A counter was set up in the corner where coffee, hot dogs, and candy bars were sold. I was sure it was colder inside than out. This was obviously a game played in places where normal people shouldn't spend time.

There were about twenty people huddled around a small electric heater, which put out just enough to warm the person closest to it. Six of the folk were immediately recognizable by the colorful t-shirts pulled on over their sweaters, identifying them as the Royal Bank Blues and the Amyot School Tigers. Two more shirts were handed out, and I became a temporary Tiger. There is a limit to what I will do in the cause of love, and this was pushing it.

Elena quickly explained the basics of the game, which sounded like a cross between lawn bowling in slippery shoes and housework with all that sweeping.

Everybody seemed ready to start but was waiting for an old man with a pail of water to walk back and forth on the ice sheet, sprinkling drops on its surface.

"Is that some sort of a blessing ritual?" I asked.

"He's pebbling the ice," Elena whispered, "so the rocks will slide more smoothly."

I was going to ask her why she was whispering until I realized she was a bit embarrassed to let anyone know that she had brought a total curling idiot to the event. So I nodded my head sagely and stifled the rest of the stupid questions I was going to ask.

Finally, both teams gathered at one end where all the rocks were clustered. At both ends of the sheet, large targets of concentric colored circles were frozen in the ice. At this point, the leader of our pack of Tigers, who was called Skip, was outlining his strategy. I eventually learned that was his title, sort of like Captain, rather than his name. I listened carefully to his game plan and instructions, and it kind of made sense, but I had no idea how it applied to me. When I asked Elena, she replied that he wanted me to throw my rock as a guard.

"To guard what, and why me?"

"Because you throw the first rock."

"Terrific," I thought, another chance in a long string of such situations for Dusty Sherant to make a total fool of himself in front of a pretty girl. I stood on the line, bent down, pushed myself in the direction of the other end, slipped, and fell flat on the ice. My efforts gave the rock a mighty push toward the target. As I lay there, I just hoped it wasn't going so fast as to crash through the other end of the flimsy building. In front of the rock, Elena and another teacher were sweeping the ice like mad with corn brooms, while the Skip kept yelling, "Sweep, sweep, sweep."

The stone ground to halt three-quarters of the way down the ice. I felt foolish that my efforts were so puny I couldn't get the rock to the target area, or house, as the curling people call it. It was confusing, as our team was cheering. Elena explained that I had inadvertently placed a guard in front of the house, just as the Skip had directed.

Back and forth, the ritual proceeded with the two teams alternately sliding rocks, first to one end then to the other, trying to bump the opponent's rocks out of the house or put their own rocks closest to the center of the circles. Total points were counted after ten ends. The Tigers were jubilant. In spite of my subsequent pathetic efforts, our team had won their first match of the season. As everyone stood around congratulating each other, I noticed Elena in what appeared to be a serious conversation with a young man who had just arrived. As we left the rink, she seemed quiet and subdued. My instincts told me this was not the time to ask questions.

"You noticed the man I was talking to."

"I did,"

"That's Tom Morgan. He works out at the gas plant with Barty. He seemed like a nice guy, so I dated him a couple of times. I finally told him I didn't think it was working out with us, but he still keeps asking me out. Somehow he's not getting the message."

"Oh, I'm sure he's getting it. His ego probably won't let him accept it."

"Hmm, that sounds about right. He does think a lot of himself. In fact, most of the fellows around here think no woman can resist them."

"Elena, I want you to know you don't have to explain anything to me. I do care for you, and I enjoy being with you, but I have no claim on you."

"I know, but I want everything to be out front with us. It matters to me."

I didn't know how to answer her. I knew what I wanted to say, but so often in the past, my efforts at expressing my feelings had ended in disaster. I kept waiting for Shelly's words to slip through the door, but they didn't come. Did I will the door to stay closed? I don't know. At that point it was all very confusing.

By now, we had reached her trailer. She sat there for a minute very still, then leaned over and kissed me. I held her, and we kissed again.

"Thank you," she said as she opened the door and got out.

My mind was consumed with thoughts of this beautiful lady as I drove back to the rig through a sea of white. The wind had died down, but the snow continued to fall in large lazy flakes, collecting and bending the branches of the spruce and lodgepole pines that lined the road, limiting the visibility to the point I almost missed the turnoff.

As I drove onto the lease, I saw they were back to drilling, and parked next to my shack was a large new Airstream trailer with lights ablaze. Beside, it was a rarity in the oilfield, a truck without dents, a brand new Jeep Wagoneer. A hundred thousand dollars on six wheels had suddenly appeared during my absence. Obviously this was Luke's surprise. When I knocked on his door, he met me with an ear-to-ear grin.

"You didn't tell me you had a young woman coming up here to help you."

"What are you talking about?"

"You said you would be training a young geologist but neglected to mention it would be a beautiful young lady. You've got to be out of your mind bringing her out here to this God-forsaken country on a job with a bunch of horny men."

By now, I had the uneasy feeling Dave Stenowicz had again omitted an important detail about this job, and I began to worry about what other surprises were in store. I knew why he had not told me. He knew I would have never signed on if he had leveled with me.

"Luke, I had no idea who they were sending. I assumed it was some young guy still wet behind the ears who had just graduated. Looks like I've been shafted from the top again. Guess I'd better go meet her and get it sorted out."

"Good luck," he replied with a smirk that only added to my anxiety.

My knock on the trailer door was greeted by a vision of loveliness. She was tall, probably close to six feet, with long blonde hair and a centerfold's body. It must have been eighty degrees in her trailer, and she was dressed appropriately in skin-tight shorts and a halter.

"Hi! I'm Kellie Angleton. You must be Dusty. Mr. Slawski said you'd probably be coming over when you got back from town." She invited me in with that warm type of infectious female smile, which always puts me on edge. I took a seat on the leather sofa next to the doorway.

"I guess we both have a lot of questions," she continued. "Mr. Slawski has the idea you would be surprised to see me, but I don't know why. I thought you knew I was coming."

"I knew someone was coming, but I assumed it was going to be male."

"Oh!"

"Yeah, Dave Stenowicz either neglected or purposely avoided telling me Kellie Angleton was female."

That stopped her. She sat down quietly, and the smile started to fade.

"I guess that makes a difference, huh?"

"It could. I don't know. It depends on you. As I get it, you've got two years at SAIT in Petroleum Technology, and your Dad set up this gig for you as part of the conditions for him bankrolling the project."

I had the feeling I was probably being a bit too blunt with her, but I went on anyway.

"I wasn't overjoyed with the prospect of training anyone on a job like this. I'm a lousy teacher, and I have little patience with slow learners."

The smile had evaporated as she sat down across from me.

"Okay," she said. "Let's start over and eliminate the bullshit. I didn't want to be here anymore than you want me here. I understand that and appreciate your honesty. The truth is my Dad has been supporting me in a manner, which I don't want to give up, but it comes with conditions. I have to substitute as the son he always wanted, so I had to study subjects in which I have no interest and come to this God-forsaken place just to keep him happy. He wants me to follow in his footsteps and

GUY ALLEN

become another big businessman. You can ship me
home, but then Daddy will pull his money out of
this fiasco, and we'll all go home. Actually, that
would be good. I could get out of this without it
being my fault. But unless you do that, I'm going to
stick it out no matter what happens."

The last statement was made with a finality,
which left me without an argument. After a few
minutes of silence, I got up and thanked her.

"Okay," I said. "I'll do my job, and you can
have yourself a holiday until it's over. If you have
any questions, or by some remote chance want to
learn what's going on, ask me. Otherwise, stay out
of the way."

I left her trailer hoping the situation had been
resolved, but in the back of my mind was this
foreboding that a whole bunch of problems was just
beginning.

The next morning I found Kellie in the cook
tent deep in conversation with Danny. Big George
greeted me as I entered and nodded toward the two,
rolling his eyes as if to say, "Here we go again."

I grabbed a coffee and sat down with them for a
few minutes then returned to my trailer to run some
more drill samples. Five minutes later Danny
knocked on the door.

"What's the deal with her?" He asked as he
entered. "She's hot and sure brightens up the place.
Ellie's all pouty now that she's not the prettiest girl
on the lease anymore."

I didn't bother pointing out to him that up to
yesterday, Ellie was the only female on the lease. I
explained who Kellie was and why she was here.

"Here's a chance for you to make your true
talents useful by spending your free time with her
and keeping her out of my way."

"You're always telling me I shouldn't take advantage of these young chicks. What's different about this one?"

"This one can take care of herself. After talking with her, I'm thinking you're the one I should be worried about."

"That almost sounds like a challenge. Do I get extra pay for stud service?" He joked.

7

Big Tom knocked on my door just as I was finishing up the morning report.

"Dusty, I think you better come over and have a look at this," he said in his slow southern drawl. "We've been drilling away about seven minutes per foot, when she slowed right down to an hour for two feet then, bang, about twenty seconds a foot. We cut in about ten feet before I stopped it. I thought you might want to have a look before we went any deeper."

I thanked him, and we headed over to the doghouse. Sure enough, the drilling time recorder showed a good break, just about the depth Dave Stenowicz had predicted on the prognosis. I checked the circulating mud, but there was no evidence of gas bubbling.

"Just keep circulating until I check the samples and figure out what we're going to do next."

Kellie was walking back from the cooktent bundled up in a parka with a big fur collar as I came down from the doghouse.

"How come they stopped drilling?"

"We got a break. It looks like we might be into something interesting. Do you want to see what it's all about?"

"Sure," she replied and followed me to the shack.

The drill cuttings under the microscope showed a very porous limestone reef rock, which accounted for the fast drilling. A sample a bit higher in the section contained an assortment of tight limestone and dense pieces of chert, which would undoubtedly have slowed the penetration rate and provided a cap for any fluids or gas in the underlying porous layer.

I moved over so Kellie could have a look.

"What is it?"

"You tell me what you see."

"Does this go on my report card?"

I let that one pass as she peered through the microscope.

"You got some acid? This looks like limestone. I want to check."

I pointed to the little squeeze bottle of hydrochloric acid. She dropped a piece of the rock in the spot plate and squeezed a couple of drops of acid on it. It immediately fizzed up.

"I see a lot of little holes in the rock. That usually means gas or fluids of some kind. Right?"

"Very good. You must have paid attention during at least one class."

She grimaced at my sarcasm, but let it go.

"So, what happens now?"

"Well, we have the reefal limestone zone, which was expected, with evidence of a tight cap rock. This would be an ideal reservoir, but there are no indications of oil or gas, no kick on the gas detector, and no oil stain in the samples. The odds are that the zone is probably full of saltwater. We have three options: we can drillstem test it now, we can cut a core and have a look at it, or we can drill through it and decide what to do after we run the logs."

"What does all your extensive training and years of experience tell you to do?" She asked with a hint of sarcasm in her voice.

"I let the suits that make all the big bucks decide."

"I think we should keep drilling."

"Okay, I'll phone Calgary, and we'll find out if you have decision-making potential."

I called Dave on the mobile, and he agreed to keep drilling.

"We were expecting that reef," he observed. "This could be interesting if these other anomalies are similar."

His enthusiasm had returned with this call.

We hit total depth on Saturday afternoon. The timing was perfect. I contacted Schlumberger to send in their logging truck and got the procedures for conditioning the hole set up with Luke.

"I just got a call from the office. Kirsten and a couple of his buddies are coming up here to hunt moose next week. They want us to find out from the locals where they should go."

"Luke, I don't need the locals; I can tell Kirsten right now where he should go."

"I know, but I doubt if they'll find moose down there. Anyway, they are flying up in Kirsten's Jet Ranger on Monday."

"Are you telling me they are going to hunt from the chopper?"

"Sounds like it."

"The Fish and Wildlife will be happy to hear about that."

"Are you going to report them?"

"You bet your ass. I owe Kirsten one from a

few years back. Intelligent people would not risk hunting from a helicopter, but that alone lets him out."

"Better you than me. It could mean my job if he thought I turned him in."

"Luke, as far as I'm concerned, we haven't had this conversation."

My next call was to Elena. She wasn't in, so I phoned Barty's number. Anna Lea answered and informed me that Elena was down at the Hall, helping decorate for the dance. I cleaned up, threw on a fresh shirt and jeans and drove into town. I found Elena with a group hanging ribbons and balloons at the Community Hall. She waved as I came through the door and came over and gave me a hug.

"I tried to phone you and let you know I'm free to take you to the dance if you still want to go with me."

"I do. I've been hoping all week that you could get away."

"Great. Things out there got sorted out earlier than I expected, so I thought maybe I could take you to dinner first."

"Sure. Shall we go to the Truck Stop or the Truck Stop?"

"What about the hotel café?"

"Have you eaten there yet?"

"No," I replied. "Is it bad?"

"Not if you like airplane or hospital food."

The Truck Stop was the typical cookie-cutter setup for serving long-haul trucks with a large parking area for the eighteen-wheelers, some sleeping accommodations for the truckers, and an attached restaurant.

As we entered the restaurant, a noisy group in a

corner booth drew our attention. One of the men
was the friend of Barty's, who had dated Elena. He
turned in his seat and stared at me with a look of
open hostility. He and his friends were repeatedly
topping up their cokes from a bottle hidden under
the table. They were getting an early start on the
evening.

I sensed the tension in Elena as we took a booth
on the other side of the room.

"Please ignore them, Dusty. They're drunk."

I held her hand to reassure her before we
opened up our menus.

While we were waiting for our order, the group
got up and took the long route to the cash register,
passing by our table on their way. A couple of
remarks about 'damn oilmen' and 'big shot from the
city' graced our ears as they went by. Elena
trembled slightly as she held my hand.

"Tom's not like that when he's away from the
group," she said. "He's actually quite shy, but I
guess he wants to fit in with them. They all work
together out at the gas plant."

After we finished our meal and left the
restaurant, I half expected a confrontation outside,
but they were nowhere in sight. I did notice a
couple of new dents in the driver's door of the Land
Rover. No big deal, as there was lots of others to go
with them, but I made a mental note that Tom
Morgan and his buddies were going to be sorry for
their efforts. We drove to Elena's trailer, and I
busied myself in the living room, checking out her
music and book collections while she showered and
changed. It surprised me how similar our tastes
were in spite of our age difference. Her limited shelf
space was filled with novels by Maugham, Hardy,
Dickens, and Dostoevsky, classical authors that I

enjoyed, plus a series of mysteries from more modern writers. Beside the tape player were cassettes of the Beatles, Eagles, Dire Straits, CCR, and ABBA, as well as some classical guitar compositions. Apart from ABBA, I was also a fan of her music.

Elena appeared in the doorway dressed in a simple black dress with matching shoes and a ribbon in her hair. It was such a beautiful vision I couldn't take my eyes off her.

"Why are you staring at me? Is something wrong?"

"Far from it. If I knew you were going to look this good, I would have borrowed a suit and tie."

She thought about that for a beat then replied, "Somehow, I can't picture you in a suit, much less a tie."

The Amyot Community Hall was a large frame structure, probably about the same vintage as the curling rink. Tables and folding chairs were arranged around a hardwood dance floor with benches lining the outside walls. At one end, a five-piece band was churning out a series of barely recognizable country tunes. At the other end, some of the local ladies had set up a snack bar with an assortment of homemade goodies for sale. The place was crowded. Although no liquor was being served, it was not in short supply, and very little effort was being made to hide the bottles, which had been brought in.

Most of the tables were occupied, but as we walked in, Danny waved us over to join him and Kellie. To my amazement, Elena and Kellie hit it off right away and seemed to have much to talk about.

Groups of single fellows were gathered along

the wall on one side of the room with unaccompanied girls along the other. It reminded me of high school dances, where members of both groups wanted to hook up but had to look as if they had no interest in the others.

Danny tried to needle me.

"I hope you're not going to start a fight like the other night in the bar."

"Nice try, but Elena was there and saw it all."

"That's right. I forgot. Well, I can hold your wallet again if you need help."

Elena smiled at him, but Kellie was all questions, wanting to know what had happened.

As Danny embellished on the truth, Elena and I danced. Just holding her, I could have stayed on the floor all night. Toward the end of the fourth or fifth song, she steered me back to the table.

"Tom is coming over here," she said.

He approached a bit unsteady but probably in better shape than he was at the restaurant. He grabbed her hand and said, "Time for our dance."

"Just one dance, Tom. After that, I'd like you to leave me alone."

When the song ended, she started to return, but he held on to her. She tried to pull away, but he wouldn't release her.

"Please let go. You're hurting my arm."

"No," he replied. "I want another dance. You don't want to go back to that old man."

Before I got up, I told Danny to keep an eye on Tom's buddies in case this got out of control. Elena was still trying to pull away as I walked over. I grabbed his arm, pressing a nerve over the wrist bone until he released her.

I said to him quietly, "Tom, this doesn't have to go any further. Just go back to your friends, and it's over. Otherwise, we can all go outside and settle it."

Slowly he looked over to his group then toward Danny, who had stood up and was ready to come over.

"Yeah, later," he said.

I let go of him, and he walked away.

When I got back to the table, I could see the look of relief on Elena's face.

"I was hoping you guys would get into it," Kellie announced. "I could have taken care of one of them."

"Not a good idea," Danny observed. "This could very easily turn into a hostile crowd if it started to get rough."

I agreed with him.

"If his buddies had come out swinging, I don't think we would have had any backup. None of the other boys from the rig are here."

While Danny and Elena were dancing, Kellie kept looking at me in a strange way.

"What are you plotting now?"

"No, it's not that. I was thinking how lucky you are. You have two people at this table that really care about you. Danny totally admires and respects you, and Elena is in love with you. I can't imagine what that would be like. I don't think I've ever had anyone give a damn about me."

"Maybe you don't let anyone get past the wall."

She was quiet for a few minutes, and then said, "Maybe."

She went on, "I'm starting to get interested in what's going on out at the rig, but I've been reluctant to let you know. Your sarcasm is starting to get to me."

"That surprises me. I thought you could handle it. You can dish it out."

"I guess that's part of my wall."

Danny disappeared for a while, which wasn't unusual. What was strange was that he would abandon Kellie for the young native girl I had seen him with at the bar. Kellie didn't seem concerned and danced with a couple of young fellows who had enough nerve to approach her. When Danny returned, he took me aside and pointed to a young couple at a table by themselves on the other side of the room. I had noticed them earlier as they looked a bit out of place with their new cowboy attire.

"Jeana tells me those two are part of the bunch who are trying to recruit the natives to petition the government to get us out of here. They have been all over the Reserve making big promises about how the folks up there will be better off if the Feds make the area into a wildlife park."

"You're kidding. There's more wildlife in this room than there will ever be out there."

"They know that, but most of them are going along with it just to see what happens. Jeana thinks it's a joke."

"So, they are the ones who have been dropping trees across our road."

"Looks like it. Do you want to go over and have a talk with them?"

Kellie had been listening and chimed in, "I can handle the girl. Do you two think you can deal with her puny little friend?"

"Kellie, this is just a talk between civilized people."

"I know, but I want to sit in on it."

"Okay, but stay cool."

The couple looked a bit apprehensive when they saw the four of us approaching their table. I introduced our group and asked if we could join them.

The girl did most of the talking. She was as tall as Kellie but with curves that suggested a very fit lady. Close-cropped hair and a total lack of makeup put her out of contention for a Miss Universe shot. Her mannerisms all said, 'wilderness girl.' Her western garb was an unsuccessful attempt to fit in with the locals.

"I'm Marcia, and this is my husband, Cyril."

He certainly looked like a 'Cyril.' He was short: noticeably overweight, with thinning hair and thick glasses, a direct contrast to his wife. It became evident in the first few minutes who called the shots in this family.

I started to explain who we were, but she cut me off, "I know who you are. You're part of that big oil bunch that is trying to rob these people of their lands."

She spit this out with such anger I could see no point in offering an argument.

"I guess that's the way it must look to you. Maybe you're right."

I sensed the immediate reaction from Kellie. I had to grab her arm before she waded in. She looked at me with disgust.

"But that's not why we came over to see you. I have a bigger issue you might be interested in. If you are serious about protecting wildlife around here, you should know about this. Monday morning, a group of hunters are coming in by helicopter to hunt moose. I'm not saying they are going to shoot from the aircraft, but it is a distinct possibility."

"How do you know this?" Marcia asked.

"They are part of the same Company that is up here drilling." I knew that would get to her.

"Where are they going? Where should we look

for them?"

"I don't know, wherever the moose are. They wanted me to find out, but I'm not about to do that."

"Maybe you should. There are a few pasturing west of Amyot Lake."

I knew I had her. Now all I had to do was set the hook.

"I'm just telling you this so you can contact Fish and Wildlife to check it out. That would be a positive step you could take in helping to protect these creatures."

At this point, Cyril, who had been silent since we arrived, spoke up, "I think we should take care of this ourselves without alerting the Department."

"What are you going to do, stand on the ground, waving signs while they fly over you with high-powered rifles? Good luck with that."

Marcia flashed a look at her husband and asked, "Could you get the message out about the moose location?"

"I can, on one condition. You stop cutting down trees to block our road."

She looked at me and flashed the first smile I had seen all evening.

When we returned to our table, Kellie asked, "What was that all about? I was all set to go at her."

"I know. That's why I didn't want you over there."

"What's the deal, Dusty? You sounded like you were agreeing with that chick."

I explained to them about Larry Kirsten's proposed hunting trip.

Danny smiled, "I had to deal with Kirsten a few years ago when I was drilling. The guy is a real jerk. What do you think these people will do?"

"I don't know. It should be interesting. My

only problem now is getting the message to Kirsten about the location of the moose without him suspecting Luke or any of the drillers as being the source."

"That's the easy part," Danny replied. "I dated Kirsten's secretary, Julieanne, a few times. I'll call her at home tomorrow and have her give him a call. How about she tells him you called her."

I thought about that for a minute then replied, "I like that. He'll be mad as hell if it goes bad, but he won't be able to take it out on any of the crew."

The band had mercifully quit around midnight, and the hall emptied fairly quickly as those who could walk helped those who were too drunk. We drove to Elena's and parked in front. Barty's house was dark, but the flicker of the television was visible through the front window. Someone was still up.

"Would you like to come in for a while?" She asked. "I can make you a cup of coffee for the road."

I sat in her small kitchen as she got the coffee maker going.

"Isn't this where I ask you to wait while I slip into something more comfortable?"

I didn't know if she was serious or teasing, so to avoid making a fool of myself, I opted for the latter.

"How comfortable do you want to get?"

"How about this." She sat on my lap, put her arms around me, and kissed me hard on the mouth. We continued to kiss and finally moved to the sofa, just as the coffee maker signaled its impatience to be shut off. Slowly she got up and went back into the kitchen. No words were spoken as we fixed our coffees and returned to the sofa.

Finally, I said, "Elena, We've only known each other for a short time, but I care for you, and I don't want to rush us and have this wind up as a short-term affair. Let's take our time so that this relationship can develop."

She smiled and took my hand.

"I feel the same way. I don't want it to end ever."

As I walked down the path to my truck, I noticed a movement of the curtains in the main house. By the time I reached the gate, the front door was opened, and Barty stepped out, beer in hand.

"Oh, It's you," he exclaimed. "I thought someone was prowling around out here."

"Been to the dance, Barty. I thought I'd see you two there."

"Naw, I had to work the four to midnight. Elena, okay?"

"She's fine."

"Well, goodnight then."

8

The drive back was uneventful. Either Marcia or her buddies hadn't got around to dropping more trees, or they were going to honor our truce, at least for a while.

When I drove onto the lease, the Schlumberger well-logging truck was running a series of logs to evaluate the hole.

"Should be finished by dawn," the technician said.

So I went to bed.

The next morning the logging crew had finished packing up their gear and was enjoying one of Big George's night crew breakfasts. As long as I had known him, he always cooked up something special for the twelve-to-eight bunch. I figured even though he worked sixteen-hour shifts himself; he somehow felt guilty to be sleeping while they had to work. Not unexpectedly, there was no sign of Danny or Kellie.

"We'll have printouts for you as soon as we get back to the truck," Schlumberger's chief engineer informed me.

"That's great. Did you see anything interesting?"

"Not much. There were a few porous zones, but

they all looked wet."

"That's about what I expected. Come on over to the trailer when you're done, and I'll sign the papers and give you a number in Calgary to fax through a set."

After breakfast, I phoned Millie's office to ask her to be on the lookout for the fax, not realizing that it was Sunday, and the office was closed. When I reached her at home, she agreed to pick them up and take them over to Dave's house. I could tell she was not happy about it.

Just before noon, my truck's horn set up a racket, signaling to me that I had a call on my mobile. I expected either Millie or Dave, but it was an excited Marty Kalloch. Without preamble, he got right into it.

"They found a body up near the Mission, not far from where the canoe and camp gear was seen. There wasn't much left of it after the animals had gotten to it, just a few bones. The body hasn't been identified."

"Who found it?"

"A couple of trappers running their lines. It was in one of their cabins."

"So, how did you find out?" I asked.

"The RCMP called me. They brought what was left of the body out to LaRonge. They thought it might be Reuben, so they phoned his daughter in Prince Albert, and she told them Reuben had been working for me. They asked me a bunch of questions, and they want to talk to you. You need to call a Corporal Hansen in Saskatoon."

I dug out a pencil and paper, and Marty gave me the Corporal's number. I decided to wait until I went to town to make the call on a land line.

Dave Stenowicz phoned an hour later and told

me he had a look at the logs and couldn't see anything worth testing. He said to go ahead and abandon the hole. I put together a plugging program for Luke and the cementers and then left for Amyot.

I called the Saskatoon number from the hotel. A woman answered, and I asked for Corporal Hansen.

"This is Corporal Lucie Hansen. How can I help you?"

I explained who I was and why I called.

"I need to talk to you," she replied. "I understand you're on a drilling job up near Amyot, but can you get away and come to Saskatoon? I was given this case when the body was found, so I'm trying to get up to speed on what has happened to date. From what I can tell, you were the last person to see Reuben Delaveaux alive."

I thought about it for a minute. My first inclination was to decline, citing my commitments, which she had mentioned. However, I was hooked with curiosity and figured the time between wells would be sufficient to drive to Saskatoon and then fly to Calgary and be back in time to start the next hole.

"I'll drive down later today. We can get together tomorrow if that works for you."

"That would be great. I need some answers, and it seems you're my best bet."

The next call to Air Canada ran true to form. On any weekday, it's an adventure. On weekends, it can be a disaster. Today was no exception. After being put on hold a number of times, I finally had the opportunity to speak with someone who's IQ was greater than her age. I was able to book a flight from Saskatoon to Calgary for the next day with a return two days later. The catch was, the only direct

flight I could get left at noon for both legs of the
trip. So much for spending a leisurely weekend with
Elena. I phoned her with the bad news.

"Can you come over for lunch before you
leave?"

"Of course, I'll see you in a few minutes."

Elena had prepared a delicious macaroni and
cheese casserole.

"I didn't know you could cook like this. I am
totally impressed."

"Well, I wanted to make something special, so
you wouldn't forget about me over the next few
days. I would sure like to go with you, but I guess
I'd better hang on to my job."

"That would be great if you could come, but
maybe we can both get clear at your Christmas
break and go away somewhere."

"I'm counting on it."

Back at the rig I packed a few essentials into a
bag then called on Kellie. She stumbled to her
trailer door, opened it a crack, and invited me in.
She looked rough, no makeup, stringy hair, and was
wearing only panties and a bra.

"Have you had any sleep?" I asked.

"We were just trying to get some when you
knocked," Danny answered as he emerged from the
bedroom.

I explained a bit about the Saskatoon trip and
told them I would be gone until the next well, which
would be starting in a few days.

"Kellie, you're going to have to look after some
of my daily stuff like phoning in morning reports,
describing the rest of the samples, and finishing the
sample log."

"I'll do what I can."

"If you need help or some answers, ask Luke or

call me in Calgary. If you're really desperate, ask Danny," I said with a smile.

"Hey, thanks for the vote of confidence," he said. "Have a good trip."

Six hours on the road to Saskatoon was not the best part of my day. My choices to pass the time were my worn-out tapes or the CBC and its artsy programming. Every time the radio started leading me down the path to slumberland, I put on Bob Seger or Meatloaf at full volume. At eleven that evening, I checked into a motel on the outskirts of the city and phoned Corporal Hansen, arranging to meet with her in the morning at her office. After a warm soak in the tub, I was asleep as soon as my head hit the pillow.

Dawn rolled in gray and cold with a steady drizzle being propelled by the north wind into the faces of all those brave souls that ventured out. Finding a parking spot near the police station was futile, and my six-block trudge had a distinct effect on my frame of mind. After announcing my arrival at the reception desk, I was informed that Corporal Hansen was expecting me and would be out presently. I was directed to a nearby chair to await her arrival.

Corporal Lucie Hansen would have appeared formidable even in civilian clothes. She was almost attractive in the manner some women adopt when competing in a man's world by attempting to underemphasize their femininity as a survival device. I guessed her to be in her mid-thirties. Her auburn hair was cut short, and her face showed very little evidence of makeup. Her athletic build was emphasized by a well-tailored uniform, which accentuated a body that was obviously in excellent physical shape. When she spoke, however, her image was betrayed by her soft melodious voice. I introduced myself, and we shook hands like a couple of suits at a business convention. Her smile was a ray of sunshine showering warmth on the cold winter morning. "I want to thank you for coming down here on such short notice," she said. "We'll go down to my office, so we can talk without being disturbed."

I needed a coffee in the worst way, but since Corporal Hansen seemed to be in a hurry to get our meeting underway, I let it ride.

"I need to explain, I have only become acquainted with this case within the past few days. I was given the file last Tuesday just as I was coming back from Prince Albert for a convention here. The file was opened when those two prospectors disappeared last fall but has been on the back burner since. The discovery of this body up near Wollaston Mission got things going again, but the officers who had been originally involved have either been transferred or are busy with other cases. So, it was given to me. Now it appears that a former employee of yours, Reuben Delaveaux, is also missing. We are trying to identify the body and determine the cause of death. The remains are presently in Prince Albert. Anything you can contribute to this investigation would be welcome. Evidently you were not questioned by the other officers."

"That's right. They never contacted me. The first I heard about all this was after I got back to Calgary."

I went on to give her a description of my discovery of the claim posts and a history of my association with Reuben on this and a previous job, bringing her up to the final day he left camp.

"And you have had no contact with Mr.

Delaveaux since that day. Is that right?"

I assured her she was correct and pointed out that, on this job, I was not his employer. We were both working for Marty Kalloch.

"I'm surprised you haven't determined if this is Reuben's body. His son-in-law, Rollie, or Reuben's daughter could solve this right away."

"I contacted his daughter, but she recently had an operation and is not able to travel, and Rollie isn't immediately available. He is working over at Lynn Lake in the mine and won't be home for a couple of months."

"Okay, let's see if I can help. I've got a couple of ideas. Do you have a list of items discovered with the canoe up by the Mission?"

"I believe so," she said as she rummaged through the file.

"Yes, here it is. There was a ten by twelve canvas prospector tent all chewed up and ripped, a seventeen-foot aluminum freighter canoe, a ..."

"Hold it there!" I exclaimed. "Reuben's canoe was wooden, an old Peterborough cedar model. That definitely was not his canoe they found."

Corporal Hansen was frantically making notes as I went on to tell her, as far as I knew, Reuben did not possess a prospector tent of the size she had described.

"So," she considered," if the camp findings and the body are related, our human is probably not Mr. Delaveaux."

I agreed with her and then asked, "Corporal, how complete were the remains?"

"Most of the skeleton was intact, although there was very little soft tissue present. The little creatures of the forest cleaned it up pretty well. The medical examiner estimated death had occurred over a month ago. That is as close as they could figure it."

"Is there a detailed description or any pictures of the skeletal remains?"

She seemed puzzled by my question, but replied, "Yes, there's a series of pictures."

She handed me half a dozen eight by ten black and white photos. "Why do you ask?"

I didn't reply for a couple of minutes while I looked through the pictures. Then I found it.

"Look here." I pointed to the bones of the left arm.

"All of the fingers of the left hand are complete. This isn't Reuben. He was missing two fingers on that hand from a chainsaw accident a few years back."

She studied the photo. "So, we still have an unidentified body. At least we know who it isn't. I think we might have found one of our missing prospectors."

"Looks like a good bet," I replied.

"You have been a real help. Frankly, I wasn't expecting any answers from today. I think we could at least buy you lunch as a thank you."

My stomach was all in favor of the suggestion.

I waited while she put in a phone call to the office in Prince Albert, letting them know the body was still unidentified. When she returned, she looked concerned.

"The bosses have requested I take an assistant, fly up there, and personally check out these campsites and the area of the claim posts. I have no idea what to look for and don't know what they expect me to find, but I have to give it a try."

"Have you ever been up there before?"

"I went on a fishing trip a couple of summers

ago. It was beautiful, but the bugs were terrible."

"Well, it will be a little different now. This is November, and winter comes early in that country. If there is any amount of snow on the ground, you won't find anything, and it will be extremely difficult to get around. You need to check out snow cover before you plan this trip. Just call one of the aviation companies up there and get their read on conditions."

She thought for a minute then replied, "If it's a go, could you come up with us and help find these sites?"

The idea of returning to the Foster Lakes country didn't fill me with enthusiasm, but the mystery of what happened to the two prospectors and Reuben did intrigue me.

"I have a few days between wells. I need to fly to Calgary this afternoon to look after some things, but I can be back here tomorrow and would be available the next day if you set it up. One day should do it if we get an early start."

"I'll see what I can do and call you tonight either way."

Luncheon with Corporal Lucie Hansen was a joy. Her transformation from an efficient RCMP officer to a sweet, friendly lady was almost instantaneous. We talked and laughed, shared backgrounds and experiences, and just enjoyed the two-hour lunch.

"Dusty, you have a plane to catch, and I have to get back to work. This has been fun," she said as she got up from the table. "I'll call you tonight."

The Calgary flight got me in just after dark. I took a cab to the apartment and immediately dropped into bed with hopes of some peaceful sleep. I was dropping off when Corporal Hansen

phoned to let me know there was no snow cover as yet south of Yellowknife, although some was expected soon. Her supervisor was insistent she visit the scene before real winter set in, so our trip was on. She had booked me into a hotel at Government expense and would pick me up early the following morning.

The next day started as one of those clear Calgary events that most of the locals look forward to after a blizzard. Mr. Cheerful on the morning radio bubbled all over in anticipation of an afternoon Chinook wind, which would lift the temperature into the balmy upper thirties. On waking, I realized I hadn't told Millie I was coming back. Out of habit, I picked up the phone to call her, thought about it, and decided I didn't need or want to talk to her today. Everything was up to date, and there was nothing to report but the rig move. I did phone Marty and relayed my discussion with Corporal Hansen and the planned trip. Marty's first question, as would be expected, had nothing to do with the mystery.

"Is she a looker?" He asked.

"She's attractive, but not pretty or cute, and probably not your type."

There was one person I did want to see. Jeremy Prince and I had gone through high school together and graduated from the same Geology course at the University of Western Ontario. We had been in continual competition in sports, academics, and dating pretty girls during those years. Jeremy had a very sterile home life with parents who didn't quite manage to fulfill the basic parental obligations. Shelly tried to do the same for me, but Jeremy and I relied on his Uncle Fred for the guidance we craved. I envied his stable environment, and he envied my freedom. Often since graduation, on my mining exploration contracts, I would hire Jeremy as an assistant if he was available. He had tried the suit and tie role at a major oil company for several years, but his inability, like mine, to play the corporate game landed him in a dead end job upgrading maps. He subsequently quit and went to work at a community college as a petroleum technology instructor, a position he presently occupied. I called his number, and the Department secretary informed me that he had a scheduled break between eleven and twelve. I left a message that I would be there at eleven to take him for lunch.

At six feet, Jeremy towers over me by a couple of inches. His once rock-hard body had softened over the years of a semi-sedentary life, but he was still in reasonably good physical condition. The Prince gene pool, however, had not been kind to his scalp, which was prematurely and totally without hair. His casual dress of jeans, loafers, and a white dress shirt, which had never seen a tie, was his trademark. Whether in the bush, the boardroom or the bar, that is what he wore.

"Is this a business meeting, or are you just lonely?" He inquired. "Since you committed to springing for lunch, I suspect the former."

We walked up to Sixteenth Ave. and grabbed a couple of sandwiches at a little bistro with outside tables. The Chinook had arrived as promised, creating almost shirtsleeve temperatures.

"So what's going on?" Jeremy asked.

I explained briefly about the drilling program and added, "I've got this blonde airhead up there who I'm supposed to be training. She claims to be one of your graduates. Her name is Kellie Angleton."

Jeremy said nothing for a beat, looking at me quizzically.

"Yeah, I know Kellie. She graduated last year, and my friend, I think you are being had. She is far from an airhead. She graduated with top marks and is one of the brightest students I've had in class in the past ten years."

He paused and then added, "And she is an excellent actress. I understand she did a lot of stage work back in Toronto. I went to a school production of 'Who's Afraid of Virginia Wolff?', and I figured she did a better job than Elizabeth Taylor in the movie."

"Hmmm," was my only reply as Jeremy continued. "Her old man's a big shot investor down east. Kellie works for him, checking out projects he's considering for investment. She explained this to me one day when she was trying to get some insight into how the oil exploration business works. Evidently Daddy has invested some money in your project. She made a strange request. She wanted the name of the person whom I considered to be the best wellsite man in the business. I gave her yours."

"Well, that explains a few things but leaves me just as confused. It would appear that she was sent up more as a spy than a trainee."

"Maybe not. Obviously, she's checking out the operation for Daddy, but I think, knowing her as I do, she wants to learn all she can of the day to day operations."

"If that's true, why did she show a total lack of interest in the beginning?"

"It was probably part of the act to set up the dumb blonde image. She read you on first contact and realized if she came on as the eager young trainee, she would never learn anything from you.

She would sense your hostility to her being there. I would guess she slowly dropped that façade, as she could detect you were beginning to accept her and start showing an interest in what's going on."

"That's interesting you make that observation because that is exactly what she has done."

Jeremy went on. "I'm also guessing she has hooked up romantically with one of the more knowledgeable members of the drilling crew. This girl uses her sexuality to get what she wants."

"You sound like you're reporting a firsthand experience."

"Not me, but one of my co-workers got taken for quite a ride by her. It destroyed his marriage, and I don't think he's over her yet."

We sat for a few minutes and finished our lunch in silence. Then I asked my friend, "How do you think I should deal with her? I don't have the time or the inclination to play a bunch of mind games."

He thought for a minute then answered, "I would be totally out front with her. Tell her what you now know about her and find out what her agenda is. I think she'll be honest with you as long as she can see being successful. If you try and snow her, she's bright enough to see through it."

We parted company with the promise to get together when I got back for some fishing in the spring.

Back at the apartment, I was reviewing our conversation in my mind when the phone rang. It was Millie.

"Dusty, why didn't you tell me you were coming to town?"

I mumbled some excuses about a last-minute decision, plane connections and other lies.

"I found out from this babe who is phoning in the reports. She said you were going to Saskatoon, but I figured she was confused, and you were coming to Calgary."

"Well, actually, I was in Saskatoon. The decision to come home was last minute."

"Why? What were you doing in Saskatoon?"

I felt a sudden touch of resentment at this last question, much the same as the instances when my absentee mother had demanded accounts of my actions during my teenage years. Every time she had made one of her infrequent trips home, she would demand an accounting of my time since her last visit. She had even at one time suggested I keep a log of my activities, which she could examine. That really set me off, and I began making up the most outlandish records of my time, creating scenarios that disturbed her to the extent that she proceeded to check them out. On one occasion, I intimated I had impregnated the daughter of one of her enemies. Another described being suspended from school for hitting a teacher. After the final report in which I reported a two-week stay in the local jail, she decided she didn't want to know any more. Checking out all my stories to find them bogus had been too embarrassing.

It wasn't any of Millie's business why I had gone to Saskatoon. Probably it was just a passing interest on her part, but this mothering aspect of her nature was beginning to get on my nerves.

"Just some police stuff," I replied.

"I must say, Dusty, your little girl assistant has an attitude. Are you sleeping with her?"

That one pissed me off. I did a ten count before I answered.

"Millie, if I thought it was any of your

business; I would give you an answer."

The next sound was that of the phone on the other end being slammed into the cradle.

I felt a little remorse for my reply because what had once been a wonderful relationship was rapidly going sour. My only concern now was whether she would be prepared to continue handling my business end of this project until its completion.

9

About an hour after Millie had hung up, Luke called me from Amyot.

"What the hell did you do to set Kirsten up? I just had to bail him and his buddies out of jail. He is fuming mad and blames you for it. Also, somebody shot a bunch of holes in his chopper. He blamed the Wildlife boys for it and really pissed them off. It's going to cost him a lot of bucks to make this go away."

"Luke, it is better you don't know how this went down. Just tell him you have no idea what he's talking about."

"Yeah, well, at least that will be the truth."

Ten minutes later Kellie called. "Boy, did you ever miss a great show. Danny and I went out early this morning and parked on top of a hill north of the Lake. We spotted a couple of moose grazing in a marshy area beside the water. Just as we were getting settled in, a truck drove up to the south end and parked. Nothing happened for a while, and we were beginning to think it was a no go. Then we heard the helicopter coming in from the west. It hovered over the moose just long enough for someone to open the door and shoot. They dropped both animals before they landed. As soon as they hit the ground and were out of the chopper, this truck drove up beside it, and that little guy we talked to at the dance got out and put about a dozen shots into the motor of the chopper. Then he jumped in, and the truck took off with our brave hunters firing at it."

"Are you sure it was Cyril who did the shooting?"

"No question, but it gets better. The pilot kept trying to get his machine started, while his buddies were cutting up the meat. In the midst of all this, the boys from Fish and Wildlife showed up and arrested them. Luke had to go to town and bail them out. I got the whole show on film. I shot everything with my telescopic lens, so you can make out license plates and recognize the players."

"That's great. Why don't you run down to Meadow Lake and get two sets of prints of everything. These pictures could solve some of our problems."

"I was thinking the same thing when I took them."

Since I had booked the return flight to Saskatoon that evening, I had the rest of the afternoon to kill. It was a good time to visit Dave and see what other bits of information he had neglected to pass on. He was in when I called, and I sensed that he was a bit unnerved to hear I was in town.

It was my turn to be surprised when I entered Emily's downstairs store. Either sales had been very good, or she was going out of business. The antiques and curios and the whatevers that used to cover every inch of floor and wall space were now in short supply, and no one seemed to be minding the store. Upstairs, I opened the door to Dave's offices and was greeted by perky little Pamela, occupying the receptionist's desk once again. Pamela's employment had been terminated a year or so ago by Dave, who cited her inherent ability to screw up even the simplest of tasks. Millie had told me it was Emily behind the termination. Now, here they were, Emily apparently closing up shop, and Pamela back. Interesting.

"Mr. Stenowicz will be right out," she announced as she pressed the wrong intercom button, attempting to summon him from an empty office down the hall. When she finally got it right, Dave was out immediately to greet me. Not wanting to get into the intricacies of the female personnel changes in the building, I let it go.

"How come you are in the city? Are we having problems up there?"

"Were you expecting some? I'm beginning to anticipate surprises from you. Why didn't you tell me Kellie Angleton was female?"

He thought for a minute then replied, "I figured if you had known you were going to be training a young female, you would never have taken on the project. As I said, your services were specifically requested, so I had to make sure you came on board. Isn't she working out?"

"She's okay, but I think she has a different agenda than just learning the intricacies of the operation."

I reiterated what Jeremy had told me about Kellie.

Dave got up, walked over to the window and stared out at the busy street below before he answered, "I told you I had a group of investors, when in fact, the truth is there is only one, Martin Angleton. He may be representing a group, but that

I don't know. He is the only player I have met. He has complete control of the financing. I submit weekly budgets to him, and he writes me a cheque to pay the bills. It does sound like Miss Kellie was sent up there as a spy to make sure the operation is legitimate. Angleton has total control and can shut us down at any time by cutting off the funding. I've been upfront with him about the wildcat nature of this play, so there shouldn't be any problems in this regard."

"I hope you are finally leveling with me. Are you sure I'm not in for some more surprises?"

"Not from this end."

"Well, I guess we'll just have to keep Daddy's little girl happy until this is over."

I had missed my noon plane but was able to catch the last flight back to Saskatoon. I booked into the hotel and was fast asleep by midnight. During the night, as predicted, a strong Arctic Front had moved south with gray skies and colder temperatures. Saskatoon's version of Mr. Gloomy on the morning radio warned of an impending blizzard. Since his prediction was for the next forty-eight hours, I wasn't too concerned but realized that we were definitely going to have to make it a fast trip. We needed to get in and out of the bush today if this was going to work. As she promised, Corporal Lucie Hansen showed up promptly at six.

As we drove to the airport, I could see she was a bit nervous.

"Are you worried about the weather?"

"Kind of worried, but there's been a slight change in plans. I guess it's just the two of us today. My partner got pulled off on that double murder, which took place last night. Consequently, I wanted to call this off, but the boss said 'no.'"

"Okay. We have to expedite this as quickly as possible today. Did you charter a plane with LaRonge Aviation?"

"Yes. They have a Cessna 180 set up for us to fly into Lower Foster Lake."

"I want you to call them back and tell them we want Johnny Greneau to fly us, and we need to land on Jenny Lake as well."

"Why?"

"Jenny Lake is a small lake much closer to those claim posts, but it's too small for most pilots to tackle. Greneau is the only one I know that will try it. He can land on and take off from a mud puddle."

"Okay, I'll make the call from the airport."

The short flight to LaRonge was uneventful, although Corporal Hansen was quiet and still seemed nervous. I tried to reassure her but without success. She was dressed for an Arctic excursion, wool shirt, and lined jeans covered by a heavy fleece-lined coat. A wool toque and fur-lined mittens completed the ensemble.

"I think you're a bit overdressed."

"I've heard it's really cold up there, and I want to be ready."

"Okay, but it's not going to be that cold."

Johnny Greneau was ready to go when we walked onto the Company dock. He tossed my big pack into the back of the aircraft, and then gallantly assisted Lucie to the seat next to him.

I stretched out in the back as we bounced our way down the lake until the floats cleared the water, and we were airborne. Conversation was somewhat limited over the sound of the motor, but I was able to direct him on a straight course to that section of Lower Foster Lake, where the two prospectors had originally been dropped off. Greneau set his heading, and with the map on his lap, pointed out the various lakes to Lucie. After what seemed like forever, I could see the chain of Foster Lakes stretched out in the distance. As we came nearer the lower lake, I had Lucie pull out her map and show him the spot where the prospectors had been landed. Johnny dropped the aircraft down smoothly, landing into the wind and pulled up along the shore, where the remnants of the partly completed camp could still be seen. Lucie and I hopped out of the aircraft and had a look around the site while Johnny tethered the plane to a couple of trees.

"There's sure not much to see. I expected some equipment lying around or some food cached up in a tree," she observed, "One thing I can't figure out is why they would leave their camp like this and head out into the bush to stake those claims. It would make more sense to finish the camp first. Is this what it looked like when you first saw it?"

"Like I said, I haven't been up here this year. I used this spot as a temporary camp a few years ago, but I haven't returned since. The first I heard about this was after my job was over, and I was back in Calgary."

"But, I thought you found their claim posts."

"I did, but that was over to the southeast by Jenny Lake. Marty and I didn't put the two events together until we met in Calgary."

"Oh, so what do you think now that you've seen this?"

"I believe..." I paused. "I'm not sure, but I believe what we're seeing here are the results of a camp that was in the process of being torn down, not partly built."

"What makes you think that?"

GUY ALLEN

"You're remark about it not making sense for them to charge out into the bush before their camp was set up got me thinking. What if the camp was set up and later torn down? So, I started looking around for some signs, which would indicate a different interpretation. Here, check these out, three small holes arranged in a regular pattern where pegs appear to have been driven in to hold the tent, which I'm guessing was probably the one found with the body up near the Mission. Those charred rocks thrown over there were probably arranged as a fire pit here over these bits of ash. And behind this ash, inside the peg holes, the ground is much smoother, where it was trampled. This would be the area the tent covered. It's about right for a ten by twelve."

Lucie had a look at my so-called evidence, took some pictures, and finally said, "That does make sense, but are you confident with that conclusion from what you see here?"

"Not totally confidant, but I can buy it better than the theory the camp was just being set up. Sure, some of these signs could be from former camps. This is a logical spot along this stretch of the shore, but the point is, you need to have an open mind about it."

"Yes, I get that, but something still puzzles me. If this was the tent area, as you say, and it makes sense because it certainly is more smooth and level than the surrounding area, why would they leave that big rock inside?"

I had noticed the rock before. It was about the size of a soccer ball and almost as round. I was a bit puzzled, but it didn't seem important until she mentioned it.

"It just doesn't look natural in here," she

110

continued as she bent down and pushed the rock over.

"Look, the area beneath it has definitely been disturbed. Let me have your hammer for a minute."

I handed her my rock hammer, and she began to scrape away the loose dirt. A couple of inches down, the pick end of the hammer struck something that, after some more serious digging, proved to be a small metal box. Carefully she pried it open. Inside were a few coins, a pocket watch, and an identification bracelet. The inscription read:

Lucien Veneau

Chicoutimi, Quebec

Lucie examined the contents, then asked, "Why would they take down their camp and leave this here?"

"I can come up with a whole bunch of answers to that one."

"Try me on one or two."

"I would guess that it wasn't Lucien that tore down the camp and left, or he would have dug this up and taken it with him. So the culprit is probably his partner, Richard, or a person or persons unknown."

"So whose body was found in that cabin with the tent and canoe?"

"I would guess it is whoever did this, Richard, or an unknown third person."

"Okay, where is Lucien?"

"It's a deep lake, Lucie."

It was just a short hop over to Jenny Lake. Johnny looked at the map and then down at the outline of the lake.

"This is going to be an adventure. Isn't this the same slough I dumped you off at last summer? I was kind of hoping I'd never have to come in here again. It's gonna be a bit of a bitch today. We're riding in with a crosswind, so hang on."

Johnny laid the aircraft in like a baby in a cradle. He taxied over to the big flat outcrop rock at the east end of the lake, where he'd dropped me off before. It was the only suitable spot. The rest of the lake was surrounded by marsh.

"I guess that's it," he said as he handed me my backpack. "Hopefully, I'll be back in just before dusk to get you. I've got one more run to make first. Just cross your fingers that this weather holds."

After Johnny had cleared the trees and was out of sight, Lucie said, "That word 'hopefully' bothers me. Do you think there's a chance he won't be able to get us tonight?"

"In this country, there's always that chance. Any time you come here, you have to be prepared for the unexpected."

"Are you prepared? I'm certainly not."

"There's enough survival stuff in my pack for two or three days, or even a week if we stretch it."

"Oh."

Before we set off to find the claim posts, I convinced Lucie to leave her big heavy coat with my pack, which we hung in a tree. I remembered traveling to the claim post as a tortuous meander through swampland. Corporal Hansen definitely found our journey much more of a challenge than walking the streets of Saskatoon. After a couple of missteps into swamp holes, which filled her boots, I cut her a walking stick to probe the ground before charging onto it. All in all, she was pretty well soaked, and her new outfit was adorned with rips and tears by the time we got to the first claim post. Patches of blood had soaked through her clothing from cuts and scratches on her legs and arms. The only good part of the walk was the absence of the millions of biting insects, which adorn the area during the warmer parts of the year.

The claim post was still in place on the small knoll where I had found it, with blazed trees running for about a hundred feet to the south. Then there was nothing. We walked the line along the ridge to the last blaze.

"This is as far as I went when I was here this summer. I don't know if they continued the line and put in the final post."

"Let's walk it and find out," she replied in a small voice that told me she really didn't want to go any further.

"I'll walk it, and you can stay here and dry out. I'll come back and get you if I find anything."

"No, I'll come along. I couldn't feel much worse, and I don't see too much chance of drying out. I'm not going to feel any better until I'm home in my warm bed."

We followed the same southerly bearing as the blazes for about a thousand feet, where we found a few more blazes and the remnants of some topolite thread. This led us to another tagged post, with the same inscription for CBS 5638, staked Aug. 2, 1985, by L.Veneau. Below that tag was an initial post tag for CBS 5639, with a series of blazes continuing south.

"Looks like they started on a second block," I observed.

I looked at Lucie. She was half-sitting, totally dejected, leaning against the post and was a mess. Her wool shirt and jeans were soaked clear through. Somewhere in the bush, she had lost one of her mittens and her toque. The bleeding appeared to have stopped, but her hair was plastered down and sweat was pouring off her. I made the offer again to leave her there and follow the blazes. I said I would come and get her if I found anything. This time it seemed to really anger her.

"I'm going to see this through. I'm not giving up just because I got a little wet."

We followed the line marked by the occasional blaze for about a quarter of a mile. Here we found another post, untrimmed, with the tags lying unmarked at the base.

"How do you figure this?" She asked.

I thought for a minute, considering under what conditions I might do the same thing.

"They probably decided they had just enough time to get back to camp before dark and figured they would pick it up and finish the job the next day."

"But they didn't."

"No. Something must have happened during the evening, or the next day to change everything. Anyway, we also are running short of time. We need to get back to the lake as soon as we can. These clouds, which are blowing in from the north, do not look good."

Our early afternoon excursion along the claim line was a walk in the park compared to the trek back to Jenny Lake. I was tempted to try a cross-country short cut but scrapped the idea when I realized we would not have the ridge to follow and could possibly miss the lake altogether. We were now walking into the face of this north wind, which seemed to be getting stronger with each step. By the time we got to the first post, it was spitting a few drops of rain as the clouds got lower. At Jenny Lake the cloud base was only about thirty feet above the water surface, and the wind was still blowing across the lake. Lucie and I stood out on the edge of the outcrop and took it all in. I could see she had reached her limit. Her clothes were torn, and she had more cuts on her legs and some on her face.

"We are probably in for a long night," I announced. "I don't think even a duck would try to land in this."

I thought she was going to cry, but she took a few deep breaths and asked, "What do we do?"

"We find some sheltered area back in the woods: gather some dry branches, get a fire going, and hopefully get you dried out, patched up and warm."

"Are you sure Greneau won't try to land today?"

"Not unless he's totally out of his mind, and I'm not sure I'd want to take off with him in this."

"So, we're here for the night."

"I guess unless you know of a Holiday Inn nearby."

Again, she had to fight back the tears.

Fifty yards in from the shore was the site of my old camp. It was sheltered and on dry ground, a small open meadow surrounded by a grove of spruce. Fortunately I was able to collect a supply of dry wood and had a strong fire going after a few minutes. Lucie moved as close to the blaze as she could without getting burnt.

"I've got an extra pair of pants and a shirt in the pack. You're going to look kind of funny, but the fashion police seldom make it out here. You need to get out of that wet stuff, put them on, and wrap yourself in that big coat of yours."

"Don't you need them?"

"No. I didn't try to swim through the swamp."

I had an old tarp in the bottom of my pack. I

dug it out and Lucie helped me tie it to enough trees to partially shield us from the wind and rain.

Dinner was a soup thrown together from some of the dry ingredients in my pack mixed with lake water. That, with a couple of cups of strong coffee, partially eased the discomfort. I cut some spruce boughs and laid them out for sleeping areas under the tarp. I offered Lucie my sleeping bag, but she was adamant in surviving the night using her own resources, which in this case consisted of rolling herself up in my spare blanket and her heavy coat and stretching out close to the fire. I zipped into my bag and was asleep in minutes.

During the night, the wind picked up, the temperature dropped, and it started to snow. We awoke to the same gray blanket of clouds and marshmallow size snowflakes, providing us with our own blankets of white.

Lucie's mood was much improved. She was dry and warm enough to entertain the hope of delivery back to civilization. I heated a mélange of instant oatmeal, lake water, and sugar, which tasted surprisingly good. I suppose, at that point, anything edible would seem like a gourmet meal. After she finished eating, she planted herself on the rock and waited for the sound of the plane. I stowed most of my gear and started to take down the tarp, but another look at the unchanging weather conditions made me decide to wait until I heard Johnny coming in. Instead, I went and sat beside Lucie on the rock.

"He's not coming in, is he?"

"I don't know, but it doesn't look promising. There's no space between the bottom of the clouds and the top of the water. He wouldn't be able to see the surface until it's too late."

"I'm sorry to have dragged you up here. I truly didn't expect it to be like this."

"It wasn't your fault," I replied. "You were ordered to come by someone sitting in a nice warm office right now. I could have refused, but I wouldn't have felt right if you had to come up here alone. I know what this country can be like, mean and unpredictable. I was stuck at Neyrinck Lake for ten days one time waiting for an aircraft."

"Why do you put yourself through this? I imagine you could get a good job somewhere more desirable."

"You're the second lady this month to ask me that question. It's difficult to explain. There is certain purity in dealing with the natural world. It's an escape from the politics and bullshit of the corporate environment. Out here, if I have a job to do, I know the obstacles and chances of success. I guess it all boils down to the freedom to be true to yourself."

"I think I understand. Many people would like that freedom, but their need for security overrides it. I know I would like to run my own investigation business, but I'm afraid to give up the security of my job to do it."

"Lucie, you're starting to look sad. We need to lighten up. Would you like fresh fish for dinner?"

"Sure, as long as I don't have to dive in there to get them."

I dug my drop line and a little tin box of hooks out of my pack. I also found an old can of Hereford Corn Beef left over from the summer to use as bait. I attached some to the hook and gave her the rig.

"It's your turn to supply the food. Throw it out as far as you can, then pull it in."

Her third try landed a little twelve-inch pike.

"Okay, you got the baby. Let's go catch the big fellows."

I cut a strip along the side of the little fish and threaded it on the hook.

By the time darkness shut her down; Lucie had half a dozen good-sized pike and a lake trout. She was having so much fun I didn't have the heart to stop her when she had caught enough for our meal, and after all, who was going to arrest her for no license.

We had to walk farther to find enough dry wood for a fire to cook the fish, but it was worth it. They were delicious, especially the trout.

We talked until the fatigue from the day took over. I was surprised to learn that she was only three years younger than me and was due to collect her twenty-year pension soon.

"That's when you need to start your business," I said. "Let your pension support you, and you can do whatever you want."

"I know, but it scares me."

We gathered up our beds under the tarp. I offered her my sleeping bag again, but she was insistent on looking after herself.

During the night, the north wind blew off the blanket of gray and brought the fury of its own blizzard. The temperature dropped about twenty degrees. I was oblivious to the change until Lucie prodded me awake. She was shaking uncontrollably.

"Dusty, the tarp is gone, and I'm soaking wet and freezing. Can we get the fire going?"

I peered out at our winter wonderland. The ground had a two-inch covering of snow, and the north wind was blowing more in. It was obvious that resurrecting our fire in this would be impossible. I explained this to her, realizing she had come to the same conclusion.

"If you can suspend your concerns about modesty, you need to get out of those wet clothes and climb into the sleeping bag with me. It's the only way you're going to get warm tonight."

She was too cold and wet and shivering too hard to argue. Quickly she peeled away the wet garments and slipped naked into the bag beside me. I held her close, transferring as much of my body heat to her as possible. After half an hour, she finally stopped shaking and started to relax. After another half hour of lying together, we made love.

10

The morning was still and cold. Snow lay as a fine, even powdery blanket covering our campsite. We were awakened at dawn by the drone of the Cessna coming in to land, causing us to scramble out of the sleeping bag to face the day. The memories of the previous night fading into the back reaches of our minds. Fortunately, I had stuffed my clothes in the bag with me the night before to keep them dry. I was able to dig another pair of pants and a shirt out of my pack for Lucie. We were an odd-looking couple that greeted Johnny as he taxied the aircraft up to the outcrop.

"I'm glad to see you two survived the storm," Johnny greeted us as he climbed down off the float. "There was no way I could have gotten in here. I was lucky to land back at base. The visibility was practically zero. We're fortunate we got a break this morning, or you could be here for a week. There's another system coming in later today, and it sounds like a serious storm. Let's get loaded up and out of here."

The trip back to LaRonge was smooth, with the sun shining through a clear sky. Johnny had brought along sandwiches and a big thermos of hot coffee,

AMYOT

which was much appreciated. Lucie was unusually
quiet as we waited for our charter back to
Saskatoon. Finally I turned to her and said, "I think
we need to talk."

"I know. I've been thinking a lot about last
night. Yesterday was a shock. I wasn't expecting it
to be so tough and to have so much trouble dealing
with it. I've always been proud to feel I'm totally in
control of my life. I've seen a lot of lousy stuff in
this job, and sure, it has affected me, but I've been
confident I could handle anything. The last two
days were so bad. I lost my confidence and acted
foolishly, and what made it worse was that you
were completely at ease through the whole ordeal. I
felt so useless. Last night I don't know what came
over me, but I needed your comfort, like a little girl
wanting to make sure everything was going to be
alright."

Her emotional confession startled me. I had her
pictured as a tough lady cop, which probably
influenced my lack of sympathy for her plight in the
swamp. I felt kind of bad, as I could have made it
easier for her, giving her lots of warning beforehand
of the perils and discomforts of our trek.

"Don't beat yourself up over this. Your first
day in this country couldn't have been spent under
much worse conditions. You came up here not
really knowing what to expect, and when you got
dumped on, you experienced the fear of not
knowing if you were going to get out. You say I
was calm, but you need to realize that I've spent a
lot of time up here under all kinds of conditions. A
few years back, I was stuck in my camp alone for
two weeks through a series of storms, short of food,
and constantly wet. I guess I've just got hardened to
it. As brutal as this country can be, it can be just as

121

beautiful. When the days are warm, the insects are under control and the fish are biting, there can be no better place on earth. You need to come up here and spend a week when it's like that."

"Maybe someday. I'd like that," she replied, "but not until yesterday's memory has totally faded. And about last night, I don't know what to say."

"You don't have to say anything; it was natural and just happened, and it is only our business. No one else needs to know anything about last night, but it was beautiful."

"Yes," she smiled.

The flight back to Saskatoon was uneventful. Lucie was much more relaxed and even dropped off to sleep for a few minutes before we landed. We said our goodbyes, and she promised to keep me posted on any new developments.

Fortunately, I had plugged my truck in at the airport parking lot, so it started right up, although the temperature had edged steadily to below minus twenty. I stopped on the way out for groceries and extra gasoline in case I couldn't get through to Amyot. With additional warm clothing, an Arctic sleeping bag, a camp stove, a lantern and the rest of my survival gear, I felt I was ready to go.

Elena slipped in and occupied my thoughts as I headed north. I could hear her excited questions. "What did you do? Where did you go? Did you miss me?"

What would I tell her? Situations like this in the past were not a problem. I was never concerned enough to spare anyone's feelings by glossing over the truth, but the realization that I did care about Elena and didn't want to hurt her, put it all in a different perspective. I could tell her about the night spent with Lucie, and she might understand if I explained the conditions. Then Shelly's words came back, telling me to be upfront and honest about everything if you care for someone. "Sure," I thought, "and look how that ended for you."

The blizzard hit when I was about sixty miles south of Amyot. For the past two hours, I had been driving through flurries, which increased as I moved north. A couple of times, when I crossed areas of mobile reception, I called Elena and learned the white stuff was coming down heavy up there.

"Are you going to try and make it all the way?" She asked.

"It's about the only choice I have now. There's nothing between me and you except bush. We'll keep talking when I can make contact, but reception around here is sketchy."

When the storm hit, it was an almost total whiteout and impossible to clearly see the road.

A couple of years before, after driving through similar conditions, I had installed an extra set of headlights, pointing obliquely to the side rather than straight ahead. I was thankful for them now. They usually illuminated the line of trees on either side, helping me follow the snow-packed road. I still had trouble seeing well enough to do twenty miles an hour, and much of the time I had to go slower.

Elena kept trying to call me, but the reception was too weak for clear transmission, and from what I did hear, I could tell she wasn't picking me up at all.

The most exciting part of the trip was meeting other vehicles. At the height of the storm, I couldn't see the lights coming until they were almost on top of me. Both of our vehicles would slow to a crawl as we passed.

My arms ached from the tension. Although

visibility continued to deteriorate, stopping was not
an option. I had no idea what was following me.
The only thing I could be reasonably sure of was
that, if they were traveling faster, they would be in
the ditch by now. I had the heater blowing full blast.
Even so, jets of Arctic air were finding their way
into the cab.

A call from Elena got through about an hour
and a half into the storm.

"Where are you? Are you still moving?"

I informed her that, according to the odometer,
I was probably about thirty miles out.

"It's bad here," she continued. "I can't even see
Anna Lea and Barty's house from my front
window, and the wind is shaking the trailer. I'm
worried about you. Please keep in touch with me."

For the next hour, I was able to continue my
snail's pace. By that time I was able to pick up a
radio station that kept up its continual warnings
about the severity of the blizzard.

I knew I was getting close to Amyot, as I began
my progression up the hill about a mile south of the
town entrance. I also remembered the slope down to
the entrance was a bit steep.

About halfway down, I felt the truck beginning
to slide sideways toward the shoulder. I feathered
the brakes and spun the wheel against the direction
of the slide, hoping to come to a stop, but the lateral
movement continued until I felt the right wheels
drop. Momentum carried me until I was completely
off the road onto a relatively level portion of the
shoulder. Attempts to move the truck either back or
forward met with failure, burying the wheels deeper
in the snow and muck with each attempt. My
vehicle was not going any farther tonight. I had two
options. Common sense and the advice of safety

experts suggested I should remain with the vehicle until help came, especially since I would be able to keep warm. However, Elena was waiting for me a mile away. Common sense wasn't an option.

I pulled on an extra heavy sweater under my parka, an extra pair of socks, my winter gloves, and my goggles. I managed to get a final call through to Elena, telling her I was going to try and walk the rest of the way. I then set out a couple of pylons, locked the truck, and headed down the road. The wind was brutal, continually stinging my face with ice crystals. I wrapped a scarf around my head so that only my eyes were exposed. The air temperature must have been pushing thirty below with a wind chill making it even colder. All I could see was a few feet ahead. I tried to pick up my pace, but the surface was slippery, and keeping upright became a problem. A couple of falls and I was covered with snow, which began to melt with my body heat, finding tiny crevices of unprotected flesh to thoroughly chill me. It seemed like I had been slogging along forever, and each time I fell, it took a greater effort to get up, as I began to feel a heavy mantle of fatigue overtaking me. I just wanted to lie down and go to sleep. Forward progress became a slower conscious act of just putting one foot in front of the other and mentally resisting the urge to rest. At the bottom of the hill, I thought I saw a flicker of light. I stumbled toward it, veering off the roadway. Fortunately, my trek led to the main street. Realizing where I was, gave me energy, and I was able to cover the remaining few blocks to Elena's trailer with a renewed sense of purpose. The door burst open before I had a chance to knock, and she was in my arms.

11

Inside the trailer, the furnace was blasting out hot air, but I couldn't stop shaking. She helped me out of my snow-encrusted garments, which were now dripping all over her floor and stationed me in front of the heat vent. Even then the shaking was uncontrollable.

"You need to get into a warm bath," she observed. "Wait here until I fill the tub."

It took half an hour in the hot water for the shaking to stop and to actually feel the warmth spreading through my body. I guess I had dozed off, for the next thing I knew she was shaking me awake. She led me to the bed, slowly disrobed, and slid in beside me, wrapping her arms and legs around me. I kissed her softly, and that was the last thing I remember until the next morning when I was awakened by the smell of fresh coffee and the sound of a snowplow clearing the road out front. The previous evening seemed like a long distant memory of a series of events, which had happened to someone else. As I slowly made the steep climb to consciousness, Elena was pouring two cups of coffee. I reentered our world.

"How do you feel?" She asked.

"Kind of spaced. I don't remember much after I left the truck. It just seemed important to keep walking until I got here."

"You must have been in bad shape. After all, I lured you into my bed, took off my clothes, climbed in with you, and all you could do was go to sleep."

"I can rectify my negligence before you head off to work."

"Hmmm, you're in trouble. The school is closed because of the storm. So you've got all day to make it up to me."

She let her robe slip from her body onto the floor. She was wearing nothing. The exquisite beauty of her body was greater than I had ever imagined in my fantasies. As she slipped under the covers next to me, I could feel the warmth of desire throughout my body. Tentatively at first, we held each other. Her skin was warm and satiny to the touch. Our bodies stiffened as we were overcome with desire. Finally, we came together in a complete union.

Nothing was said as we held each other tightly until the ringing of the phone shattered the moment. Slowly we untangled as she reached over for the receiver. It was Danny. Reluctantly, she handed it to me as I sat up on the edge of the bed.

"Everyone has been looking for you," he began. "I figured you were either at Elena's or frozen solid in some ditch. Luke said to tell you if I found you that we're just about done surface hole and should be running casing tonight. Kellie has worked out a casing program, and Luke checked it out, so you're off the hook for a little while. What do you want me to tell them out here?"

"That I'm frozen dead in the ditch. It should give me a couple of days."

"Yeah, I'm sure Kellie will be glad to hear that. She's starting to bitch about being overworked."

Thoughts of the job, or pretty much anything else except Elena, were far from my mind, but unfortunately, reality had crept back in. Finally, I responded. "Just tell them I'll be coming out tomorrow. I need to get my truck towed and thawed out before I can go anywhere."

"What a shame," he replied. "I can imagine how badly you want to leave that warm bed and come out here."

"Well, I guess that's the start of our day," Elena observed.

"Not quite," I replied, coaxing her back into bed, where only the hunger for food around noon got us up and about. I phoned the truck stop, which had the only tow truck in town and told them where I was stuck.

"You're not the only one in the ditch on that stretch of road. We'll be down there in a couple of hours and get you all out," the driver replied. I told him I'd come and get the truck in the morning.

The lease area for the second well was located in a broad valley flanked by a moderately steep ridge running roughly parallel to the trace of a small intermittent stream, which meandered its way along the valley floor during the warmer months. The rig was set on a level spot near the base of the ridge. The whole area in the valley was covered with sedges and wetland grasses, now frozen and completely covered with snow. In summer, this would be a muskeg and virtually unsuited for any activity involving heavy machinery, but winter brings the frozen ground, which is fully supportive to all types of equipment. Toward the crest of the ridge the change in vegetation was gradual with thick growths of bushes and vines covering the slopes. The ridge summit was lined with stunted patches of spruce.

The newly plowed lease road was an adventure in spine-jolting travel. These were the times I wished I had replaced the springs and shocks in the old Landrover, but it was running well and didn't seem any the worse for its night in the ditch. This morning it was in much better shape than I was. Sleep, in Elena's company, had not been a readily available commodity last night. Somehow, discussion of the events of my night by Jenny Lake didn't come up. This morning we awoke to the alarm and arose unsteadily to face the day. After breakfast I ventured out to shovel the walkway out to the road but discovered it had already been done. I walked Elena to the school and then continued to the truck stop.

Luke was up in the doghouse when I arrived. Surface casing had been run, cemented, and the crew was waiting for the cement to set before drilling out the plug. He greeted me as I climbed the stairs.

"Nice to see you could join us for morning coffee. When we heard you were driving up here through the storm, we thought we'd have to send some St. Bernards out to find you. It's just as well you weren't here. Kirsten showed up the day before yesterday mad as hell and looking for you. He had arranged for a truck to come from Edmonton to load up the helicopter and take it back for repairs. When they arrived, the chopper was gone with no sign of it anywhere. He had the local cop out, but they have no idea where it went. Somehow he has it in his head that you are responsible for all this."

"He thinks I stole his helicopter? Come on, Luke; even Kirsten can't be that stupid. I wasn't even here."

"I told him that, but he still thinks you're involved."

"Well, it looks like you survived the storm."

" Yeah. We had to shut down here for about four hours, and then it took another four to dig out."

I agreed that it was a storm of substance.

"You didn't tell me that helper of yours was so sharp. She figured out the whole casing program without any help. I checked it out. Hell, I've seen graduate engineers that have had trouble doing it."

"Luke, I'm learning a lot of interesting things about that girl. At this point, nothing would amaze me."

When I opened the door of my trailer, I was surprised to find everything had been unpacked and set out as before. Kellie was sitting at the desk, peering through the microscope.

"You must be bored," I observed, "spending your time looking at drill cuttings."

"I figured I'd better learn this crap if I'm going to end up doing all the work around here."

"Okay. That sounds about right. Now, shall we start over?"

"No, I think we are about even."

"Kellie, you did a great job while I was gone, and Luke commended you on your casing program."

"Well, thank you. It's not rocket science, and I'm sorry I pissed off your secretary, or whatever she is."

"Don't worry about it. I've been doing the same. I think Millie's about ready to quit anyway, which wouldn't break my heart. She's starting to become a pain."

"I guess I shouldn't judge her until I meet her," Kellie replied.

"You probably will once we're done here."

"I can't wait. What is she to you?"

"She used to be someone I was very interested in. Now she's just a lady who does my secretarial stuff."

"Did you lose interest in her when you met Elena?"

"That and a few other things, which happened along the way."

"Oh! Am I being too nosy?"

"Yes, but that's okay. It's all history."

"Your Millie intimated we were sleeping together."

"I know," I replied. "Did you set her straight?"

"No, I thought I'd let her sizzle."

"Kellie, did you know that Jeremy Prince and I go back a long way? We had lunch together when I was in Calgary. Can you guess our main topic of conversation?"

"I'd like to think it was hockey or sex, but I'm guessing it was all about me."

"Among other things. I wasn't aware you were so talented. I've come to the conclusion you have a way different agenda than I was led to believe. Do you think you could level with me as to why you are out here?"

"Okay, it's no big deal," she replied. "As you probably know, my dad put up most of the money for this play. He has always been wary of investments of this type, but this one was so far off the wall it appealed to him. He did a thorough check on Stenowicz and was satisfied that, although the guy isn't popular, he's legit, but he wanted me to check out the people out here and the day-to-day operation. I asked Jeremy to recommend a wellsite geologist or engineer, and he picked you, so I had Dad insist that you got the contract."

"Is your father acting alone in this, or is he fronting a group of unidentifiable investors?"

"You mean is he laundering Mob money? The answer is 'no.' I know most of his backers, and they are legitimate businessmen with a bunch of money to put into weird deals like this."

"Just what did you expect to find out here?"

"We really didn't have a clue. Dad just wanted me to make sure there were no cover-ups, money wastage, or shoddy performance."

"Look, Kellie; you're going to find all of those problems to varying degrees on any drill job. This isn't a cookie-cutter type of operation. The only thing you can expect is the unexpected, and screw-ups are a regular part of it."

"That's what I've come to believe. I held off reporting anything for the first couple of weeks until it occurred to me the whole operation is organized chaos."

"Not even necessarily organized. So, where do we go from here?"

"I'm through spying," she replied, "but I would like to stay until we finish the job."

"And what about Danny? Are you playing him too?"

"I was at the start, but I've grown to care for him. He's crazy and fun to be around, and I like to be with him."

"You know he's got a wife and three kids back in Edmonton?"

"He told me, and I just don't know. If it's not a problem for him, I don't want to know about their relationship."

"Okay, if we can be honest with each other and quit playing games, I'm willing to take on the tutoring bit, if you want to learn and take over part of my job responsibilities."

"Why, so you can spend more time with Elena?"

"That, and if we do screw up, I can tell your father it was your fault."

"Dusty, I don't screw things up."

"Uh, huh. You're too young to be perfect."

"Okay," she replied. "I'm in, but one other condition, no more sarcasm."

"You really want to take the joy from my life, don't you?"

"No, but sometimes it hurts."

"So I'm finding out. I'll try and back off, but there are times I can't resist."

"Okay, but try harder."

"Oh, I almost forgot. Did you get the pictures developed?"

"They're in my trailer. I'll go get them."

When she returned, we went through them together.

"These are great close-ups," I observed. "I can recognize the faces and read the plates. If you ever get sick of looking through a microscope, you could make a living with that camera. These shots of them shooting from the chopper and Cyril pumping bullets into it are beautiful, and the one of the boys from Wildlife arresting Kirsten, I want that one on my wall when he shows up."

"He was here the other day looking for you. You're right about him being a jerk. The minute Luke introduced us, he started coming on to me."

The next morning Kellie and I drove into

Amyot for breakfast at the truck stop. Seated near the front of the restaurant were Marcia, Cyril, and another couple. After we had found a booth, I walked over to the group and invited Marcia to join us for a few minutes.

"Why would I want to do that?"

"Because I have a couple of bits of information that could change your life."

"I doubt that," she replied but got up and walked over with me.

"Okay. What's all this hot information?"

I didn't reply. I just handed her the picture of Cyril firing into the chopper.

She took a full minute to examine it, her face getting redder with each passing second.

While she continued to stare at the photo, I announced, "The Company that owns the helicopter has hired some private investigators out of Edmonton to find out who inflicted this damage on their aircraft, and who stole it. They'll be up here in a day or two to locate the culprits. I'm sure they would find this photo most interesting."

"So, I suppose you're going to give it to them."

I thought for a minute, then replied, "Not necessarily, if we can reach an agreement."

"What did you have in mind?"

"You lay off interfering with our operation and quit trying to turn the natives against us, and I'll bury the pictures. I don't care what else you do here; just get off our backs until we pull out."

"We can do that."

"Don't you have to get your partners over there to agree?"

"No. They do what I tell them. You keep up your end of the deal."

"No problem. By the way, what did you guys

do with the chopper?"

"We had nothing to do with that. A bunch of the locals loaded it onto a flatbed that night and hauled it away. We have no idea where they stashed it, but we heard they're going to try and sell it back to the owners when things cool down."

As she got up to leave, I handed her the picture.

"Give this to Cyril with my compliments. He can hang it on his wall to remind him of his big moment in life."

Kellie had been silent throughout the discussion, which, in itself, had been a surprise.

"When did you hear they were sending detectives up here to investigate?"

"I didn't. It just seemed like a good idea."

The next day I drove into Meadow Lake and had some 'Wanted' posters made up with Kellie's picture of Kirsten being arrested enlarged to cover most of the page. The caption at the bottom read 'Wanted by the Saskatchewan Moose Association.' I posted one in my trailer, one in the Amyot Post office, and one in the doghouse. I sent the rest to Kirsten's secretary for distribution around the office. Luke took down the one in the doghouse.

"Are you trying to get me fired?" was his only response. I noticed he did, however, save the poster in his filing cabinet.

Two days later, a brand new Mid-Continent truck pulled up in front of Luke's door. I didn't pay any attention to it until Larry Kirsten barged into my trailer.

"You son of a bitch! You set me up."

I waited a beat then replied, "How about you go back outside and knock on my door like a normal person, or is that too tough?"

He ignored my suggestion and continued his

rant.

"I finally figured it out. You sent down word where those moose would be then told Wildlife we were coming after them."

"Well, not exactly. I told a bunch of environmentalists, and they told the Government boys."

"Who shot up my chopper, and where the hell is it?"

"That's the part you will have to sort out on your own. The word I get is that some of the locals have your helicopter stashed away. I wouldn't worry about it. I hear they are about to offer to sell it back to you. Evidently it won't fly."

I could see Kirsten getting madder by the minute.

"I'm going to get back at you for this. You're going to learn not to screw around with Larry Kirsten."

"I wouldn't be in too much of a hurry to get your revenge if I was you, I may not be done messing with you yet."

"What does that mean?"

"When do you go to trial?"

"In a week or two, but my lawyer has that under control. Wildlife doesn't have much of a case. They didn't actually see what happened, so they've got no proof. We fully expect to beat the charge."

"You might want to rethink that," I said as I handed him copies of the pictures Kellie had taken of him firing his rifle from the open door of the helicopter.

"Where the hell did you get these? Did you take them?"

"Afraid not. I was down south at the time."

"Who took them?"

"Do you really think I'm going to tell you? Why don't you pass these on to your lawyer? If he can convince me that you will plead guilty and happily pay your fine, I won't send these to the Government. I'm sure they would love to have them."

"I think you're bluffing. These pictures won't make any difference even if you do send them."

"Do you want to take that chance?"

Kirsten stomped out, still convinced he could beat the charges; however, he did take the pictures with him.

We settled into a much more harmonious routine. Now that Kellie was no longer trying to delude me with her dumb blonde act, I was continually surprised at the depth of her knowledge and abilities. By degrees, she took over the role of supervising the sample collection. The crew members assigned to collecting and cleaning the drill cuttings were generally those with the least rig experience and the lowest level of intelligence. Luke referred to them as his 'posts' because, as he explained to me, they were as dumb as posts when it came to working around the rig. I had been a bit lax with them, generally doing the final wash myself in order to save the fine material and make the cuttings useable. Not so with Kellie. First, she went to Luke and demanded a brighter group of rig hands to perform the task. Then she instructed them in the cleaning procedure she required and threatened them with the loss of their jobs if they didn't measure up. Somehow she had sweet-talked Luke into backing her up. After a few days, one of the group quit and stated that if he was going to take that kind of crap from a woman, he would go home to his wife. But surprisingly, by the end of the week, things had settled down, and the sample quality had improved dramatically.

I had mixed feelings about the changes. I welcomed the reduced workload and the opportunity to spend more time with Elena, but a few embers of lingering doubt and suspicions about Kellie's agenda remained.

By the third week in December, we were getting close to the total estimated depth for this hole. A thin gas-bearing sandstone zone had been picked up higher in the section, but I had decided to delay a test decision until we had a look at the porosity and fluid content logs. Kellie had described an increasing number of granite chips over the last twenty feet, making me suspect that we had drilled into a granite wash sand on top of the granite basement rock. This new zone was hard and slow to penetrate and dulled the last bit after fifty feet of drilling.

Thursday morning was another clear and cold one, with the mercury edging down below minus thirty. A quick look out the trailer window showed the boys were still running into the hole with the new bit. I had spent the previous evening with Elena and didn't get back to the site until 3 AM.

As I stepped out the door, the first sound I heard was not the roar of the rig but the crack of a high-powered rifle. The next sound, a split second later, was that of the bullet slamming into the side of the trailer inches from my head. I dove under the Landrover as the second shot tore into the side of the truck. Two more shots kicked up snow beside the vehicle. Then silence. I stayed where I was until I heard more shots but much closer and from a semiautomatic. I peeked out from under the truck to see Big George standing outside the cook tent firing at a grove of trees about two hundred yards away at the top of the ridge. No movement appeared near the target, and George quit firing after a dozen rounds. I took a chance and did some broken field running over to his position.

"Did you see anything?" I asked.

"Yeah, somebody in a parka up by the edge of the trees. He took off as soon as I started shooting. Didn't get a look at his face, he was all bundled up."

"Have you got your Skidoo running? I think we should go up there and have a look."

"Sure," Big George replied. "But get your gun; he could still be up there."

I went back to the trailer and grabbed my Magnum while George was cranking up the snowmobile.

To get to the top of the ridge, we had to run up the valley floor to the point where the slope to the top was gentle enough for his old machine. Snow had started to fall as we left camp and was coming down heavy by the time we reached the grove of trees a half-hour later.

"Whoever it was is long gone," George observed. "See the tire tracks running off over there?"

The faint tracks were rapidly filling with snow.

Suddenly the sound of another shot blasted the stillness. The bullet glanced off the metal treads in a shower of sparks. We hit the ground as a second shot thunked into a tree behind us.

"Can you see him?" George yelled.

In spite of the snowfall, I could just make out the form of a vehicle on the edge of the trees about a hundred yards away.

"Yeah, give me your rifle."

I fired three rapid shots and was rewarded by the sound of bullets striking metal. As I looked up, I could just make out the vehicle moving out of range.

"It sounded like you hit him. Could you make out what kind of truck it was?"

"Not very well. It looked like a light-colored van of some kind."

"Well, there's no point in trying to follow him in this weather," he continued. "Sounds to me like that bunch of tree-huggers are still trying to make trouble for us."

"Maybe, but I don't think so. It's not their style to deliberately try and kill someone. Those first shots were meant for me personally. This is something else, but I don't know what."

George had picked up a trail of footprints from the track to the edge of the ridge from where the first shots had been fired. He scuffed the snow around where the prints ended.

"Can't see any casings here. Either he gathered them up, or they're buried. Probably wouldn't help us even if we did find them. Are you going to call the Mounties on this?"

I had thought about it on the way up and decided there wasn't a lot of point, as the ineptitude of the local Constable was a topic of humor throughout the area.

"No, I don't think so. The chances of Charlie Baker solving anything around here are limited."

As I answered, George was kneeling beside the fast disappearing vehicle track.

"Dusty, what's this orangey stuff? It looks like some kind of pollen or powder off the trees."

"I can't really tell from this," I said, examining a handful of snow with a few flecks of color. "I'll take some back and check it out under the microscope. It wouldn't be pollen at this time of the year. It almost looks like little flecks of paint."

By midmorning, Big George had regaled everyone who came within earshot with the events of the day, embellishing his story each time he told it. By early afternoon things had more or less settled down to normal.

I was just completing the daily report, when Kellie came in, checking out the bullet hole in the trailer wall.

"Have you figured out who you pissed off bad enough to shoot at you?"

"You were my first choice until I remembered you were still sleeping when it happened."

"Couldn't have been me, I wouldn't have missed. Any other suspects?"

"I've got a couple of ideas who it could be."

"How about that Moose fellow you took down in the bar? Danny tells me he's back in town. Maybe it was Marcia and her posse, sort of payback from Cyril for that picture."

"Those are possibilities, and I also want to check out Elena's old boyfriend and his pals. It's the kind of sneaky thing I'd expect from them. Right now, I don't know."

I told her about the light-colored van we saw on the ridge.

"I'll ask Danny if he knows anyone with wheels like that."

She then pulled a couple of sample vials out of her pocket and poured one in the microscope tray.

"This is the first five-foot sample since they got back on bottom. I haven't had a close look at it, but it appears to be all granite, angular pieces, and no rounded stuff. It looks like we're in the basement."

My first casual look at the cuttings through low power was a bit of a shock and brought me back for another look at a higher magnification. It confirmed my first impression. Pieces of a mineral, which I didn't expect to see and shouldn't be there, were definitely in the sample. I looked at Kellie, but she was busy leafing through a magazine and wasn't aware of my excitement. I was surprised and a bit suspicious that she hadn't noticed the change. Finally, I turned and said to her, "You're probably right. It looks like basement rock, but I think we better cut a bit more to be sure."

She looked at me quizzically.

"You're kidding. That will take the rest of the day. How can it not be granite? Nothing else drills that tough."

Thinking quickly, I replied, "Sure, it's granite, but it could be more granite wash, the sandy deposit weathered from the granite, and carried into a lower area. There could be more sedimentary rock below."

I could see she was not convinced, but she said nothing at first.

Finally, she sighed and said, "Well, I guess it means I'm stuck here. I was going to go to town and do my laundry and meet Danny when he gets off shift."

"Go ahead; I'll look after finishing up."

I could see she was reticent to go, but probably her desire for the rest of the day to herself was in conflict with her curiosity as to what scheme she suspected I was up to. Eventually, she left. I watched her drive off the lease before I proceeded to gather up all the drill cuttings I could locate from this last bit. I switched the bags of samples destined for the Government Conservation Board with those from the actual unmineralized granite. I set the shale shaker to catch everything, which came across the screen. Only Vince Capolchuk, the driller, questioned why I wanted to cut so much granite, but I thoroughly confused him with some complicated meaningless scientific explanation, which seemed to keep him from asking any more questions. I had decided to keep drilling within reason until we got through this new stuff.

By midnight, we had cut another ten feet. The new mineral was still showing up in samples, although in decreasing amounts. By three in the morning, we had another five feet and were back to pure granite. I used this barren material from the bottom of the hole to fill all the sample vials and bags so that, as far as I knew, any of the mineralized material was stored safely in my truck. There was one small package I planned to send to Jeremy to get analyzed. I gave the orders to stop drilling and to condition the hole for running logs. I called for the logging truck and went to bed, thinking. "How often do you get shot at and make a possible important mineral discovery on the same day?"

12

I awoke to a morning of bright sunshine and cold, cold air. Yesterday's snow clouds had moved east. The logging truck was on-site, and nobody was shooting at me. It had the potential for a good day. Today was Elena's last teaching day before the Holidays. She had agreed to come out and stay with me until the well was finished before she went to Edmonton to spend Christmas with her family.

When I returned to the trailer after breakfast, Kellie was stretched out in the recliner reading my sample log.

"You sure cut a lot of granite."

"So I've heard."

"How come?"

"Like I told you, I wanted to make sure we were in the real stuff."

I was beginning to get irritated with the questioning from Kellie, then Capolchuk, later from Luke and now again from Kellie.

"Any more questions?" I snapped.

"Yeah! What's with the sulphur in that dish of water?"

"What?"

"On the table, those little grains of sulphur."

I had forgotten about the powder we had found in the tire tracks on the ridge. Sure enough, on examination of the yellow grains under the microscope, there was no doubt it was sulphur.

"Don't tell me you found that in the granite as well. Where did they come from?"

I explained to her about the tracks. "The only place around here that I know of to find sulphur is out at the gas plant. I think they have a small scrubber, which cleans out any sulphur in the gas before it goes into the pipeline. Maybe the shooter works out at the plant."

"What about your two candidates? Do they work out there?"

"I don't know about Moose, but Tom Morgan and his buddies sure do. I figure I should have another talk with Mr. Morgan."

"Can I come along? I'd still like to see you punch him out."

"No, you're too eager to see me get beat up," I replied. "Hopefully, we will just talk."

With the loggers running a full suite of logs, I figured it would be late afternoon before they had printouts. There was time to have a talk with Tom Morgan before I picked up Elena.

The gas plant was located east of town on a treeless wind-swept field. It was essentially a main collecting station where the natural gas from a number of nearby wells was scrubbed of minute concentrations of hydrogen sulphide then pressured up into a branch of the main pipeline, which ran from this general area of Northern Saskatchewan south to the major population centers and eventually hooked up with a line into the United States.

A Quonset hut served as the office, where a young receptionist, who didn't look old enough to be out of high school, greeted me, "Can I help you?"

"Sure, I'm looking for Tom Morgan. Is he on shift?"

"He is, but he's out at one of the wells."

"Can you tell me where?"

"I'm sorry, I can't. He's looking after several wells, and I don't know which one he would be at right now. Can I take a message for him?"

I hesitated, then thought, "Why not."

"Tell him Dusty Sherant would like to talk to him. He can reach me at this number."

I wrote down my mobile number and gave it to her.

I drove to the school and picked up Elena. We went over to her trailer, where she packed a few necessities, set the heat so the pipes wouldn't freeze while she was away, and locked the place up. We were on the way to the wellsite when my mobile phone rang. Expecting an update call from the rig, I was surprised to hear Morgan's voice.

"The girl in the office said you were looking for me. What's going on?"

"I don't want to get into it over the mobile line," I replied. "Can you meet me?"

"If we make it quick. I'm on my way home to get cleaned up for a party tonight."

"Okay. Meet me at Elena's in ten minutes."

We turned around and headed back to town. Elena was nervous about the whole thing until I explained that I just wanted to talk to him.

Tom was waiting in the yard with Barty as we drove up.

"What's going on?" Barty demanded as we came through the gate.

"No big deal. I just need to talk to Tom for a

few minutes. Why don't you come along? Maybe, you can help me out here."

Elena unlocked the trailer and invited us in.

The three of us trudged in and found seats in the small living room while she put on a pot of coffee. I went through the events of the previous morning and the tie-in to the gas plant from the sulphur grains in the tire tracks. I described the vehicle I had seen up there as best I could.

"I considered you as a possible suspect, Tom, but Elena assured me it couldn't have been you."

"I wouldn't shoot at anybody," he replied. "I don't hunt. In fact, I don't even own a gun, and furthermore, yesterday, I worked the eight to four at the plant. You can check it out."

"What about anybody else, maybe one of your buddies? You all work there."

There was no reply for a few minutes, until Tom said, "Look, half the folks around here have either worked out there or made deliveries. None of my friends would pull a stunt like that, or I would have heard about it. As far as light colored vans, I can think of at least a dozen just in town. Besides, it would take weeks to check out all the tires that roll on and off that property. I don't see how I can be of much help to you."

Just then the truck horn went off, and I had to rush out and take an update call from the loggers. When I returned to the trailer, both men were getting up to leave.

"Moose has been working as a fill-in driver, when one of the regulars is off," Barty observed. "I saw him out there last week, but I don't know about yesterday."

"Can you check it out?"

"That stuff is supposed to be confidential, but I

can find out. I'll let you know."

On the way out to the wellsite, Elena asked if I was going to check out Tom's story.

"No, I believe him."

When we arrived at my trailer, Kellie had the log printouts spread across the desk and was studying them intently.

"So have you got it all figured out?"

"I wish. Either we didn't spend enough time on this stuff in the classroom or the lab, or I missed a few of the classes. It's not making a lot of sense. I stacked all this electronic stuff up against our sample descriptions, so maybe I can recognize how the different squiggles on these charts compare with the different rock types, but that's about it."

"Okay. Let's go through them together. The loggers made three runs, each with a separate electronic tool, and each measuring different characteristics of the rock zones adjacent to the tool as it was pulled slowly up the hole. We're going to be looking for a number of things from these runs: the type of rock in each level, locations of formations and zone marker horizons, the presence of any potential oil or gas horizons and characteristics of the rock zones such as porosity, permeability and contained fluids or gas."

I pointed out the different curve shapes between a tight siltstone bed and an adjacent porous sand stringer that had appeared in the samples. By now, I had total attention and apparently understanding from both young ladies.

"Does that mean this will be a gas well?" Elena asked.

"We won't know until we run an actual test on the zone," I replied. "The sandstone is only about one meter thick, so it will depend on several other factors such as: whether the gas is under high pressure, whether it can move easily through the rock and how far the sand extends. It may be just a local lens or the edge of a major gas-bearing reservoir."

"So, if you can get most of this information from one run, why do you need these other logs?" Kellie asked.

"It is mostly for backup data and to further define rock characteristics more precisely."

"A lot of this seems redundant," Elena observed. "Wouldn't it be cheaper just to run the first one?"

"A bit cheaper, but most of the expense involved in doing this is getting the truck and crews out to these places and having them set up, so you might as well get as much data as possible."

For a few minutes, I let it all soak in. Surprisingly, Elena seemed to understand it as well as Kellie.

"Well, ladies, let's put you two in charge. What's our next step?"

They looked at each other and laughed.

"Wow, if I knew I would have to go to work out here, I would have stayed in Amyot," Elena observed.

"Yeah," Kellie added. "I would have joined you, but let's see, I guess I can do your job for you again. Basically, we have three options: abandon the hole, test any zones that look like they have a chance, or just run production casing and perforate that little gas sand."

"Is testing a big deal?" Elena asked.

"Usually not, if everything goes right."

"We have to test that sand," Kellie observed.

"Any other zones?"

"What about this one up here?" Elena asked, as she pointed to a similar looking sand lens higher in the hole.

"What do you think, Kellie?" I asked. "Should we test that one as well?"

Kellie looked at the upper sand zone on all the logs before replying, "I wouldn't."

"Why?"

"Well, for one thing, it's too shallow to have much pressure. It's less than half a meter thick and it has low resistivity, which means it conducts electricity, so it probably contains salt water."

"That's good. Now, do you want to set up the testing program?"

"Sure, I hate to see you overworked."

Kellie got on it right away and phoned for the testing unit to be on-site at dawn. She had methodically worked out the test interval and most of the other details. I offered to check out her results, but she was sure no errors had been made and declined my help. It crossed my mind that maybe this was the time for a lesson in humility. Anticipating some of the questions the testers would be asking, I stuck around while she made the call. The confusion was evident as she began fielding their queries.

"Dusty, they want to know if we want to run jars and if dual packers are required."

"What do you think?"

"I don't know."

Realizing the difficulty she had making that last statement, I felt a twinge of sympathy.

"Tell them we will run jars with dual packers above and a single below."

After she got off the phone, she started in, and all my sympathy dissolved.

"You knew they were going to ask those questions, and that I wouldn't know what they were talking about. You set me up. Why couldn't you have gone through it before I called?"

"I offered to, but you told me you had everything under control."

She was quiet for a beat, apparently accepting the truth of my last statement.

"I know what packers are, but why two above the tool?"

"These packers expand when you put weight on them, effectively blocking the hole around the drill pipe. Using two is just a safety measure. The mud column above the testing tool is heavy. When you compress the packers against the sides of the hole, you seal off this mud column above from the testing tool. This allows any fluids in the formation to flow into the tool when it is opened."

"And what are jars?"

This one I couldn't resist.

"Well, they are small metal cups inside the tool for catching the first fluids from the formation. Why don't you go out tomorrow morning, while they are assembling the tool and check it out?"

"Maybe I will," she replied, as she got up to leave.

During the evening, I could sense something was troubling Elena. A couple of times, she started a question and then withdrew. Prompting her to go on was of no avail. However, later she leaned over, her face within inches of mine and said, "We have to discuss something."

"I guessed that from your mood this evening."

"I know. I'm concerned that you've been wondering why I haven't invited you to come home with me for Christmas and meet my family."

"No, not really. Should I be concerned?"

"I want you to come, but I'm afraid my family will scare you off."

"Why? Are they like the Adams Family?"

"No, but they can be difficult."

She definitely had my curiosity now. Either this was going to be her way of cooling the relationship, or her folks were truly something to be reckoned with.

"Are you religious?"

Now the red flags were coming up, and Shelly's mumblings in my head were getting louder as our dialogue entered this new minefield. His voice was cautioning me to go slow.

"That depends on what you mean by religious. If you want a one-word answer, it would be no."

"Do you believe in God? Are you a Christian? Have you been saved?"

"No, no, and no."

"I'm freaking you out, aren't I?"

"That one's a yes. You're very perceptive. The truth is, it's not a subject I think about or particularly care much about."

"That's about what I thought. Don't look so concerned. I feel much the same way, except I have had it pushed down my throat ever since I was born. My parents and two older brothers are very devout, whereas my sister and I are the black sheep, holding out for a more sensible version of reality. Being with my family will probably be very uncomfortable for you. I love them because they are my family, but I spend as little time with them as possible. When I am with them, I go along with their game just to keep the peace. This is why I haven't asked you to come. I care too much about us to let them jeopardize it."

"I understand what you're saying, but the most important thing to me right now is what you want me to do."

"I don't know. I guess it depends on how you feel."

The dilemma was apparent. As close as I could tell, this was going to be one of those advance-retreat situations. Shelly's voice was almost shouting with all kinds of warnings. I could avoid meeting her folks and forgo the unpleasantness, or I could face the challenge head-on. Unfortunately, in cases like this, I suffer from the inability to fake it and go along with a charade. I sensed that Elena had figured this out, hence her reluctance to bring me along to set off the fireworks. On the other hand, I plan to be with this lady for a long time, so meeting her folks would happen somewhere down the line.

"Do you care if they don't approve of me?"

"I don't know. I've thought about it, but they don't approve of me, and I'm family, so I guess it would be nice but not realistic."

I thought for a minute then replied, "Why don't I drive you to Edmonton when we're finished here, and we can work it out along the way. I have to go home for a couple of days, so I can either drop you off or spend a few days with you and your folks."

"Okay. It would be nice to make the trip together and see if we can come to some kind of workable solution."

The next morning found the country still in the grip of the Arctic system. The thermometer read twenty-eight below with a slight breeze. Elena had left the bed just after dawn, informing me she was going to join Kellie. By the time I crawled out, the test string was being run in the hole, and the girls were nowhere in sight. After roughing out the morning report and sending it through to Millie, I found them in the cook tent in a lively discussion with Big George, Danny, and the rest of the graveyard shift. I was greeted by everyone except Kellie.

"Boy is she pissed at you," Danny observed.

"I expect she had a good look at the jars."

"That was kind of mean," Elena put in.

"What happened?"

"She asked them to show her the jars, the little cups that catch the fluid."

At that point, Kellie got up, slammed her chair back to the table, and stomped out.

"I guess I'd better go talk to her and apologize," I said as I followed her out the door. We walked together in silence over to my trailer. Once inside, I expected her to vent her fury on me, but instead, she began to cry softly. I realized I had gone too far by forgetting her bravado was a cover for an insecure young lady.

"I'm sorry. That was a mean thing to do."

"I thought we were past that. I felt so stupid, not knowing the jars were devices for jarring loose the drill string when it gets stuck. Maybe I deserved it. I guess I have been coming on pretty brash."

Tentatively, I put my arms around her, and she buried her head in my chest.

"Truce?" I asked.

"Truce," she whispered.

13

The drillstem test was successful. We measured a moderate flow of gas with good pressure readings and no salt water. When I finally got Dave on the phone, he told me to run production casing, cap the well, and release the rig until the New Year.

Two days later, Elena and I were on our way south. The trip was uneventful with a clear day and dry roads. After considerable soul searching, we decided a brief introductory visit was worth a try. I agreed to make a serious attempt to suspend my boat-rocking attitudes.

I learned both her father and older brother were preachers in a couple of evangelical churches. Brother number two was a partial family outcast by nature of following a different line of faith in studying to be a priest. Elena's description conjured up a household modeled on the Spanish Inquisition, and here I was, the heretic, entering their fortress. The whole thing was beginning to scare me. It's often pathetic what a man will do for love.

We hit the outskirts of Edmonton just after midnight and checked into a motel. We both agreed her arrival on their doorstep in the middle of the night with a strange new boyfriend would probably not be met with joy and laughter.

The family home was a three-story, gray-frame big box dating back to post World War II. It was neat and well kept with no garbage, broken shutters, or untrimmed hedges or trees. It had been painted within the past year with somber colors, which I figured was a reflection of the serious nature of the folks who lived there. The walk was freshly shoveled and swept, and a large crèche had taken over the street-side yard.

I felt Elena's hand tremble slightly as we mounted the steps and rang the bell.

"How am I doing so far?"

She gave me a sick little smile and squeezed my hand as the front door opened, and the warmth poured out.

The elegant lady that welcomed us was not what I expected. Elena's descriptions of her family had led me to picture her parents as a severe Spartan couple out of a Norman Rockwell painting. Her mother was, in fact, a classy looking lady with a good figure and an open, friendly face, a probable future image of Elena in thirty years. It was easy to see where Elena got her beauty. She greeted us warmly, hugging her daughter and shaking my hand.

We followed her into an extended vestibule, which led to a formal sitting room. Formal was the compelling theme to the point I was reticent to park my butt on anything resembling a chair. The room was large, probably occupying over half the main floor. Everything was paneled in dark wood with bookshelves filling one wall from floor to ceiling. The large windows facing the street were effective in keeping light from entering this cheerless space. They were covered with pull-down blinds, backed by heavy full-width curtains.

"Would you like some tea or coffee?" Mrs. Padrona asked as I attempted to subdue my nervousness by wandering about checking out titles on these extensive rows of books.

"That would be nice; whatever would be the least trouble."

"We'll have coffee," Elena answered, returning to the room from somewhere in the dark reaches of the house. "I'll fix it," she continued and disappeared again.

Mrs. Padrona and I sat politely, facing each other. I sensed that holding a conversation with this lady was going to test the control of my usual style of language. Picking my words carefully, I remarked on the beauty of her home, realizing the lack of sincerity in my compliment immediately. She smiled knowingly.

"Mr. Sherant," she began slowly, "I can sense your anxiety. Please relax. As you can imagine, your arrival with Elena was a complete surprise to me. I wish she had let me know, but I guess I should be used to her unexpected behavior by now. That is her nature. I'm not going to ask you a lot of questions. It is, however, my wish that you can spend enough time with us so that we can get to know you."

"I would be happy to answer any questions you have," I said. "I would also like to tell you I care very deeply for your daughter, although we haven't known each other that long."

"Are you planning to be wed?"

"We haven't discussed marriage."

"I see," she replied uneasily.

At this juncture, thankfully, Elena reappeared with the coffee. Almost at the same instant, the front door swung open, admitting a blast of Arctic air and a young man dressed entirely in black. A black overcoat, hat, and umbrella, which, when placed carefully on the coat rack, revealed the man's slender form clad in a black suit, tie, shoes, and socks. The question as to the color of his underwear passed briefly through my mind.

"My brother, Tim," Elena announced, introducing me as well. He offered his moist limp hand as a tentative acknowledgment of my presence while mumbling a greeting.

"I must rush off and finish my sermon," he said, furtively backing out of the room.

"Elena will make up your room, while I fix us some lunch," Mrs. Padrona announced.

My room turned out to be an afterthought addition on the top floor with a roughed-in bathroom down the hall. It was cozy but hot with all the collected heat from the lower levels.

"You get the whole floor," Elena announced as we trudged up the narrow stairs. "Our parents have their bedroom on the main floor; the rest of us are on the second floor."

"I guess that answers my first question."

"I know. They'd never let us get away with sleeping on the same floor, much less the same room."

"I'll live," I sighed reluctantly, "but it certainly opens up a new area of potential adventure."

I could see Elena did not appreciate my attempts at humor.

We survived lunch with mother and brother then headed to the West Edmonton Mall with the excuse of last-minute Christmas shopping. It was my first introduction to this immense monument to the Canadian consumer. It was impressive. One could easily get lost in this labyrinth of stores and boutiques, which catered to every conceivable shopper's dream.

The evening meal at the Padrona's was not one I will soon forget, much as I would like to. Dinner was formal. Elena informed me that all family members near enough to make the trip were commanded to be present. She also indicated my cleanest jeans didn't qualify as formal. Fortunately, I had brought along a dress shirt and a pair of non-denim pants. Elena rustled up a tie from somewhere to complete the ensemble.

Looking me over critically, she said, "I guess it will have to do."

Carl Padrona, Elena's father, was a man that commanded attention. Standing well over six feet, his massive body showed little evidence of an indulgent lifestyle. Although in his sixties, he was a person who kept himself in good physical condition and was very conscious of his image. Very few men have had any success in their efforts to intimidate me, but I sensed that this man was going to try. His handshake was overly firm, meant to impress. His booming voice welcomed me to his home in the name of Jesus Christ as I entered the room.

In contrast, my meeting with Elena's younger sister, Ginny, was much more pleasant. She wrapped her arms around my neck and kissed me passionately on the lips. This didn't seem to faze anyone but me. Where Elena was tall and dark with a beautiful well-developed body, her sister was short, blonde and cute. They hardly looked like sisters to the point that my suspicious mind began reevaluating Mrs. Padrona's sexuality.

The other actor in the scenario was Carl junior, a physical replica of his father but lacking his outgoing nature and natural charisma. In fact, he was the only one of the group to whom I took an immediate dislike. I sensed the feeling was mutual. I guessed one out of five wasn't bad, but the visit was still in its early stages.

Dinner proceeded better than I had expected, primarily due to Carl's running comments on the events of the season and the world in general. The food was good, and after the initial small talk and questions, I was left more or less alone except for Ginny's attempts to catch my attention. She was making me nervous, and I sensed that Elena was also uneasy with her sister's actions.

After dinner, coffee was taken in the great room, as they called it. As I sat down next to Elena on the sofa, I felt I was ready for the inquisition she had warned me about, but it didn't come, at least not that evening. Instead, the family held something they called a prayer meeting, where they held hands, bowed their heads, and listened to Carl ramble on for the better part of an hour. I went through the motions, although I had no sense of protocol for such an event. All my efforts were focused on staying awake.

By ten o'clock, everyone had wandered off, leaving Elena and me alone. She seemed to relax as the last one left the room.

"Well, that was a trip," I observed.

"I know. I'm a bit surprised at them. Either Dad has mellowed, or this is the calm before the storm. By the way," she smiled, "you faked that praying bit pretty well."

"Are you suggesting I wasn't sincere? But what I want to know is, what is it with your sister?"

Elena was quiet for a few minutes before she answered, "I didn't get into it about her because I didn't expect her to show up. She has problems, a whole bunch of problems, mostly involving drinking and sex. She's addicted to both. Mom has gotten her out of a few scrapes, mainly drunk driving and creating scenes in public places. Dad tries to ignore it, but the notoriety is having an effect on his Ministry. My brother Carl wants to have her committed to an institution, but so far, the rest of us won't go along with it."

"So, is she going to be something I'll to have to deal with?"

"I don't know. I'd say lock your door tonight, but unfortunately, none of the doors have locks."

Around midnight we regretfully parted company and headed for our separate beds.

Fortunately, or unfortunately, I'm not sure which; I wasn't surprised by a nocturnal visitor.

The next day was Christmas Eve. I awoke to another cold Alberta morning. Being on the top floor, I was soaking up all the heat from the rest of the house. The bedroom was like an oven. By the time I wandered downstairs, I learned that everyone had risen early, and only Elena remained in the house. She had prepared breakfast for the family, and we sat down to what was left.

"I was hoping you'd sneak up and visit me last night. I'm having trouble going back to sleeping alone. Not even your crazy sister was interested."

"I had a talk with her last night," she replied. "I told her if she tried anything with you, I'd help my brother put her away. That really scared her."

"So, what's our plan for today?"

"We're expected to go to Brother Carl's church this evening and to my father's service tomorrow.

Do you think you can deal with all that, or do you want to take off early, like today, and avoid the church stuff? I can fake you an alibi; say you had a prior invitation. If that's what you'd like to do, I understand."

"I want to be with you as much as possible," I replied, holding her tightly. "I'll play it out, and who knows, I might even learn something."

We bundled up and spent most of the day hiking through a park along the frozen Saskatchewan River. Along one stretch, a group of kids had shoveled the snow for a hockey rink. We watched the game for a while then took a well-marked path through the rest of the park. The silence of this snowbound world in the middle of the city seemed to bring us closer as we walked along.

"I used to come here all the time when I couldn't stand it any longer at home. It was the only place I could find peace away from the turmoil of my life with them. I'm glad I can share it with you now."

"It's a beautiful spot, even at this time of year. I can easily see why you would want to get away. I guess everyone has their own set of demons to face while they are growing up."

Brother Carl's mission church occupied the lower floor of a two-story building, part of a five-block stretch of similar buildings in the Warehouse District. During working hours, this was an area busy with trucks moving in and out. At night it was deserted except for the street people, who sought some warm shelter in the labyrinth of alleys and doorways and who comprised Brother Carl's congregation. We dressed down to fit in with the clientele and arrived early to offer any needed assistance. Brother Carl was due to go on at eight, but the folks were trooping in when we arrived, and by seven-thirty, all the folding chairs were occupied. Homeless people of all ages, both male and female, were lined around the walls.

"Is your brother really that good, to attract this big a crowd?"

"Well, not exactly," she replied as Brother Carl mounted the stage.

Ten minutes into his sermon, I was nodding off. He was the dullest man I have ever listened to. His flock didn't seem to mind, but as my senses started to pick up the sounds and smells from a back room, the whole thing became clear. These people were here for the food.

Brother Carl droned on for two hours. At least half the congregation was asleep. Snores punctuated his fiery description of the Hell that awaited those who refused to repent throughout the room. Finally, he wound down, and the main attraction, the serving of the meal, was announced. Most of the folks knew the drill and began lining up on one side of the room, as serving tables loaded with large vats of bubbling stew were rolled out to the front of the room. Elena and I pitched in with the other servers to ladle out the long-awaited meal. Brother Carl was nowhere to be seen. Elena greeted many of the regulars by name, and it was evident they were happy to see her, as they stopped and chatted. The atmosphere in the room was much improved with Brother Carl's absence.

We must have served a couple of hundred hungry souls, many coming back for second and third helpings. When it was all over, we helped clean up. We were both beat as we headed back to the house. At least we felt we had done something worthwhile.

It was after midnight when we returned to the Padrona home. Elena's father was sitting alone in the great room reading when we entered. He put his book down and motioned me to come in. Elena started to accompany me, but Big Carl indicated he wished to speak to me alone. I seated myself across from him as she proceeded into the kitchen. He was quiet for a minute or so and then said, "I've been meaning to have a chat with you, but things have been so busy at the church that I haven't had a chance until now. I hope you are enjoying your stay with us."

"Yes," I replied, "it has been pleasant. You folks are most hospitable."

"There is one thing I must ask you, as it is very important to me."

This, I knew, was the punch line coming, the moment of truth that Elena had warned me about.

"Have you accepted Jesus Christ into your heart as your personal savior?"

Elena and I had rehearsed this scene several times on the trip down and had come up with a few scenarios, which she felt would keep the peace. But I had known then, as I felt now, that I was going to have to be out front with this man. I thought about an answer for a few moments then replied, "Since I'm not too clear on what acceptance entails, it would be reasonable to conclude I haven't, and that I wouldn't be particularly interested in the process. Mr. Padrona, I am a scientist, and as such, my views are derived from theories of evolution, my personal experiences in life, and factual evidence. I have read the Bible and see it as a mildly entertaining chronicle. I do not see it as divinely inspired."

I could tell Big Carl was a bit shaken by my

attitude.

"How can you not see the beauty and complexity of life in our world as being anything but divinely inspired? How can you explain the miracles and other events for which science has no answers? How can you picture our world as a haphazard mishmash when there is so much order?"

"I can't, and science cannot explain everything, but progress is continual. Many of the mysteries and so-called miracles of a hundred years ago can now be explained, and the explanations survive scientific testing. These are things which can be observed and experienced and do not have to be taken on faith."

"Then, you would not call yourself a Christian," he countered.

"I don't use that label, and I'm not sure what defines it, although I try to live my life in line with many of the so-called Christian principles. I accept the premise that Christ lived and was probably an exceptional individual with some knowledge and abilities, which were advanced for his time. But, I believe that was all he was, a man, not a divine creation or the so-called Son of God."

"But surely you must believe there is a God."

"I'm afraid not. That is the essence of what I cannot accept. I'm sorry if this disappoints you, but I would not feel right in misrepresenting myself to you."

"It is disappointing, and it saddens me," he replied. "Although I appreciate your honesty, I was hoping we could find some common ground, and I could welcome you into our fold. I can see now it is not likely. In fact, I don't feel comfortable having someone with your lack of faith stay in our home any longer. I would like you to pack your things and leave tonight. I also request you not have any further contact with Elena. Her faith is not strong, and I can see where her continued association with you will drive her further away."

"I will leave immediately, but I will not stop seeing Elena. I love her, and I believe she loves me, and to deny this for the sake of philosophical differences is wrong."

He was about to speak again but seemed to realize there was nothing more to say. He looked intently at me for an instant, then got up and left the room.

Elena came into my room as I was throwing the rest of my gear into the duffel. I explained what had happened.

"I kind of thought that was the way it would go. I knew you had to be true to your feelings. So, I guess we go to plan B."

"I guess so."

14

I hung around Edmonton for a few days, took in an Oilers game, and looked up a couple of old friends. Finally, I picked up Elena at the bus depot on the 29th.

"So, did they buy your story that you were required to go back to work early?"

"Mom drove me to the depot, so I told her the truth, briefed out what had happened between you and my father and that I was going to Calgary with you instead of back to Amyot. Somehow she wasn't surprised. She just told me to be careful."

"At least you have one relatively sane person in your family."

She sighed and replied, "I guess that depends on how you define sane."

What was important was that we were back together. I was looking forward to our few days alone in Calgary, but when we arrived at my apartment late that afternoon, I sensed something was wrong or maybe just different. It wasn't anything I could put my finger on. It was just a series of things, which didn't seem to be in the right place. My stuff, which is generally distributed haphazardly, was somehow arranged in a strange fashion. It wasn't neater; it was just different. There were no blatant changes, but there were minor ones, which would only be obvious to me. My first thought was that Millie had been over; exercising her unique touch, but it wasn't her style. It was not the result of massive cleaning or the neurotic arrangement of everything in view. Besides, our relationship had deteriorated to the point I would hardly expect any more unsolicited effort on her part. This scenario had the signs of a careful search of the premises with some effort toward a cover-up. A cursory look around suggested that nothing was missing, but I wasn't sure. The first things I checked were the logs and reports on the wells, but they were still locked away undisturbed. I resisted the urge to call Millie for a possible explanation. With Elena by my side, I had no desire to spar verbally with Millie today.

We lay in bed until noon Wednesday, delaying the escape from the cocoon of our love. It was a beautiful day warmed by an early morning Chinook wind off the western Rockies. We dressed and planned our few days together.

Elena insisted I call Millie to try and sort out the suspected invasion of my home and maybe patch up any differences between us. Only a few months previous, I had sought out and enjoyed Millie, now she felt like a source of irritation. What time can heal, it can also destroy. Millie answered the call, "I wondered when you were going to get in touch. We have things to talk about. We may have a few problems."

Her voice came across with a formal, very business-like tone.

"Okay, let's start with my apartment. Someone

has been in here. I don't sense it was you, and I'm not accusing you."

"It was me. I was there with the police. They wanted to do a search. I couldn't reach you, so I agreed to it as long as I was present. We were there yesterday morning. I asked them not to make a mess, at least any worse than it was."

"What did they want?"

"It had to do with Faron. They've found out a lot more about her and her past. Can you believe they couldn't find anything until they checked prison records? She had been locked up for the past five years under her real name."

"That certainly explains a lot. What was she in for?"

"Dealing drugs. That's what the cops were looking for. They figured since your apartment was the last place she visited before she died, she might have left some of her stuff there."

"I didn't see anything, but I wasn't looking for something like that. All she left was a wet, ratty old raincoat. I threw it in the garbage before I left."

"Didn't you check the pockets?"

"No, I just got rid of it. There could easily have been something in the pockets. Did they take anything from here?"

"No, not as far as I could tell."

"At least they must have had some sort of document to get in here."

"No, I let them in. I thought if I was there, they would have less opportunity to plant something and then all of a sudden discover you were hiding drugs."

"Okay, it's done. Thanks for looking after it. Let's hope there will be no bad fallout. Is that it for problems?"

"No, I didn't even put that one on the list. Stenowicz is a concern. He's slowing down on making his payments. In fact, our last invoice to him is a couple of weeks overdue. I've phoned his office several times, but usually there's nobody there. When I do get through, I can never get a straight answer. There's something wrong over there."

"I'll look after it. Dave has to get the money released by Angleton before he can make payment. I'll go over and see what I can do."

"Great. I'm getting tired of trying to deal with him. Would you like to get together for dinner some evening while you're here? Tony has been asking about you."

I detected a softening in Millie's tone. The invitation to dinner was a surprise and presented a bit of a dilemma. I realized more than ever I needed to keep our relationship on a professional but friendly basis, but I wasn't quite sure how to accomplish it.

"I definitely would like to meet, but I would like to bring Elena along."

There was no reply for a few moments. Finally, the less friendly version of Millie replied, "That would be fine. Just let me know what evening you would be available."

I explained to Elena the police action and the reasons for it as well as Millie's part in it.

"I think she made the right call," Elena replied. "That girl, Faron, must have been something."

"Yes, she was different."

Apart from trying to squeeze some money out of Dave Stenowicz, it was most critical I meet with Jeremy. I had sent the granite samples to him to have assays run and hadn't talked to him since. I called him, and we agreed to meet for dinner at the Corkscrew. He hadn't received the results, but he would contact the lab and get some preliminaries.

After lunch, I phoned Dave's office. There was no answer, but I decided to track him down. This was a bit too important to let slide without putting some pressure on him. I arranged for Elena to meet us for dinner, describing Jeremy to her in case she arrived before me.

"Just for kicks," I said, "flirt with him, but don't tell him who you are."

The first floor level of Dave's building, where Emily ran her antique shop, had 'For Lease' signs plastered all across the storefront. The door was unlocked, so I entered the dark, dusty ghost of the former, brightly-lit thriving business. The mice and spiders were staking their claims on what was left.

The stairs to Dave's offices on the second level showed signs of recent use. There were footprints in the dust. This did not look good. However, to my surprise, Pamela was at the reception desk, and Dave was in his office. After she screwed up my name in announcing my arrival, Dave welcomed me to his world. He had aged a few years in the weeks since I had seen him last. He was leaning back in his chair, feet on the desk, trying to look composed, but his nervous movements belied the façade.

"I've received your reports, so I guess you are here for some money," he announced.

"That would be nice. It is somewhat overdue."

Dave slid forward in his chair and planted his feet back on the floor. He stared intently, and then his face relaxed.

"Dusty, I can give you some but not all of it. Angleton won't release any more money until he's satisfied the program is going as it should."

"What else does he need? You're giving him all the reports, aren't you?"

"Yes, of course. I can't figure out what he wants, either. He keeps putting me off every time I make contact."

I thought about it for a few minutes and then replied, "He's stalling until he gets confirmation from Kellie that all is well. She's all wrapped up in her sex life and probably hasn't reported. I can try and get in touch with her, but I haven't a clue where she went after we shut down. Just give me what you can, and we'll sort the rest out later."

Dave proceeded to write me a cheque for less than half of what was owed.

"You don't look so good. Are things okay?" I asked.

He appeared to shrink into himself before he answered, "No. Emily has left me and has hired a lawyer to start divorce proceedings. All of the kids except James, are on her side. I don't know what to do."

"Can't you fight it? If you don't, she can take you for everything you've got."

"I can't. She hired a private detective, and he got her a bunch of evidence on me with Pamela. There's nothing I can do. At least Pamela is sticking with me."

"Dave, you need to get a good lawyer and let him get you a decent settlement. You're too old to start all over with nothing."

"I know. I've talked to a couple. They've essentially told me I'm screwed."

By now, the usually self-confident Dave Stenowicz was quietly sobbing.

It was five-thirty by the time I had battled my way through rush hour traffic and reached the

Corkscrew. Elena and Jeremy were sitting at a table in the corner by the fireplace. Jeremy was in the middle of some animated story. When I walked in, Elena immediately spotted me and winked. He was oblivious to my arrival. His attention was entirely absorbed by this beautiful lady he had just met. When I walked up to the table, he got up quickly and shook my hand.

Dusty, I want you to meet this…"

I held up my hand to stop him.

"Just a minute," I said as I leaned over and received a passionate kiss from Elena.

"You were saying?" I went on.

He was quiet for a beat and then laughed.

"After twenty years, you finally got back at me. You truly do strive to get even."

To satisfy Elena's curiosity, I explained how this same scenario played out in our last year of college, only with the roles reversed. I had taken a serious interest in a young coed I had seen on campus but had not as yet met. One morning I arrived early for classes and decided to stop in for a coffee at the cafeteria. There she was sitting alone with her nose in a book. I was a bit nervous, but I sat down next to her, introduced myself, and we began a delightful conversation of getting to know each other. I was basking in the warmth of this beautiful girl's smile. A few minutes later, Jeremy walked in and took her into a passionate embrace as I was trying to introduce them. It was to my dismay that I learned they had been dating since the beginning of the term.

As the evening progressed, I realized how special it was spending time in a pleasant setting with my best friend and the woman I loved. Our conversations covered the spectrum. Elena was especially curious to learn what I was like in my younger days, and Jeremy went to great pains to paint me in as unfavorable light as possible. Fortunately, she did not believe him.

When we had finished eating and were settled in with our drinks, I asked Jeremy about the assays.

"I got some early results just after you called. All of the samples ran better than an ounce to the ton, and one ran close to three ounces of gold. There's nothing much else besides the gold, just a trace of silver and molybdenum. Where did you get this stuff?"

I explained they were drill cuttings from the bottom of the last hole.

"How deep?"

"Just under three thousand feet, definitely mineable if there's enough tonnage."

"You know, if this gets out, you're going to have a hell of a staking rush."

"I know. I'm trying to bury it. That's why I sent the samples to you. I don't know who else I can trust."

I went on to explain how I had substituted barren cuttings in the samples for the Board.

"Does Kellie know?"

"I don't know. She's the one that could spill it. She was suspicious as to why I was drilling so deep in the granite. I wouldn't be surprised if she caught on to it."

"I'd be very surprised if she didn't. She is too sharp to miss something like that," Jeremy observed. "I'm willing to bet she's playing you to see if you will level with her."

Elena had been quiet throughout the discussion. Finally, she said, "I'm a bit confused. Doesn't that syndicate that Kellie's father runs have the rights to what's there?"

It was Jeremy who replied, "I would guess they only have rights to the oil and gas under the terms of their lease. To get control of the minerals, they would have to hold staked claims or a claim block."

"How sure are you of that?" I asked.

"Not very. I know what works in Alberta, but Saskatchewan could be different. I probably should check it out for you. They know you in the mining game over there and might wonder about your questions. I would be surprised if Angleton had tied up the mineral rights, although there is an operating gold mine north of where you are. If Kellie knows about this, I'm sure she will alert her father to have the ground staked."

"You two are just talking about the legal side of this," Elena pointed out. "What about the ethics? Isn't it more important to be upfront with them and tell what you found?"

"I've been thinking about that," I replied. "It seems to be the more important issue. I've been thrashing it around in my head ever since I made the discovery. Legally, if it's open ground, as I see it, I have three options. I could spill it all out to Angleton, and he could have it staked and make another million. Conversely, I would not tell anyone and take my chances that in a couple of years, nothing would happen, and I could stake it then. Less credible would be to have a friend or associate pick it up in their name. Under normal conditions, I would just let Angleton know now, but something strange is going on with this whole program, and I'm not getting paid on time or in full. So, until the payments are up to date, I'm just going to sit on it."

"Okay, that makes sense," Elena sighed, "would you promise that you will do the right thing if and when all the debts are settled?"

"Sure, that's what I planned."

We finally found our way home and stumbled into bed after two, too blitzed to do anything but fall asleep.

The next day was New Year's Eve, the last day before we had to head back up north. Recovery from our previous evening's celebration was slow. It was afternoon before we were out of bed, fed and reasonably close to feeling human. Our first decision was that any further celebrating in observance of the New Year was out of the question.

"We could always make a quick trip to Edmonton and catch your brother's sermon tonight," I suggested.

"That's not even funny. I can't think of a worse way to start the New Year. Didn't you tell Millie you'd get together with her?"

"You're right. I forgot. I guess I'd better call and keep the peace."

Millie's office was closed, but Tony answered her home phone.

"Are you coming over to see us?" Tony asked.

"I can't make it this time. I have to go back to the well tomorrow. We'll get together next time after this job is over. Would you put your Mom on the phone?"

"She's not home, Dusty. She's out with her new boyfriend getting stuff for the party here tonight. Aren't you coming?"

"Uh, Tony, I don't think I was invited."

"Oh. Well. Good-bye," he replied and hung up.

"I guess that problem is solved."

15

Our holiday was over, and it was time to go back up north. We took two days for the trip to Amyot. The relative warmth of our time in Calgary gave way to increasing cold and snow as we crossed the Saskatchewan border and approached our destination. Although the roads were bare all the way, the snow was piled up into drifts four and five feet high in the village. Not knowing if my trailer had been moved to the new location, I stayed at Elena's until the next morning when she had to go to work. My phone call to Luke revealed that most of the crew had returned the day after New Year's and were busy clearing away the snow, so the drilling rig could be torn down and moved. Even though I would have nothing to do for a few days, I decided to drive out and check the location for the next well and make sure my trailer was moved safely. It was mid-afternoon by the time I arrived at the old drill site. The first thing I noticed was a police car pulled up to the catwalk and Constable Charlie Baker, Luke and Vince Capolchuk standing at the bottom of the doghouse stairs. As I walked over, I could see their attention was directed to a dark object lying in the snow beside them.

"What's going on?" I asked as I approached.

Luke walked over, put his hand on my shoulder, and answered, "There's been an accident. We just found Danny's body about an hour ago while we were clearing the snow away. It looks like he fell from the monkey board and cracked his head on something as he was coming down. There's a lot of blood. No way of telling how long he's been there."

I walked over and pulled the tarp from my friend's lifeless body. All of a sudden, my strength left me, and I had to sit down in the snow until the wave of nausea passed.

"When did it happen, and what the hell was he doing up there with the rig shut down?"

Luke thought for a moment and then replied," We don't know. It could have been any time over the past ten days. The Constable here says he doubts they can set a time of death since the body was probably frozen soon after impact. As for what he was doing up there, I haven't a clue. You knew him as well as I did. He did some strange things."

I turned to Constable Charlie Baker.

"Did you check up there for anything unusual?"

Luke again replied, "Constable Baker has a problem with heights, so Vince went up. He said everything looked normal."

"I guess we'd better let Danny's wife know."

"I phoned her, but no one was in. Constable Baker suggested he contact the Edmonton police and have them tell her in person."

"Yeah, that sounds right. Also, see if they can find out from her if he came home for Christmas and, if so, when he left. That might give us some idea when it happened."

Charlie Baker seemed satisfied with the plan and said, "As far as I'm concerned, this was an accident, and I'll report it as such. I'll send someone out for the body."

After the Constable had driven off, Luke observed, "If Charlie Baker is as useless as the locals say, I don't think we are going to get much help from him on this. A couple of the boys on the rig claim he gives the word 'stupid' a whole new meaning. We've got a field office in Edmonton. I'd like to get one of our boys out to talk with Danny's widow and get some answers before the police screw it up."

"That sounds good, but make sure they send someone with a bit of sensitivity. She probably has had a tough time with his running around and being away from home so much. Something like this could push her over the edge."

"I agree," Luke replied. "I know her slightly, and she strikes me as being a bit fragile."

"Something else is bothering me. Didn't you leave a skeleton crew out here to keep an eye on everything while you were gone? Surely they knew when Danny turned up."

"Yes, I did. Big George and one of the roughnecks from Amyot were supposed to stay here and check out anybody that came on the lease. When I got back, I gave them a few days off. I'll see if I can get in touch with them and find out what happened."

"In the meantime, I'd like to go up on the monkey board myself before you drop the derrick and see if I can spot anything unusual."

"Take it easy," Luke replied. "That ladder is damn slippery."

I climbed up the metal ladder slowly and very

carefully, hanging on to the side rails with each step. Everything looked normal, as Vince had reported. The restraining harness was intact, as were the bars framing the platform. Nothing appeared to be out of the ordinary until I leaned over the bar along the path, which Danny's body would have taken. If the air had been still, I would never have seen it. But the slight breeze ruffled some strands of fibers caught in a pipe connection. Carefully I extracted a few, folded them in a tissue, and climbed back down. Back at the trailer, I had to dig my microscope out of the packing box to have a closer look. They were definitely organic, either hair or fur. The strands were mainly a light gray with white portions at the ends. It wasn't Danny's hair; his was black. Somewhere in the back of my mind, an image flashed. They looked familiar, but I couldn't place the context. Thinking maybe Luke might have some idea of what it was, I called him over. He stared intently through a hand lens for a minute then looked at them under low power.

"Looks to me like animal fur, maybe rabbit or fox," he said. "You found them up there? That is strange. It would have to be some rabbit to jump that high. Probably an animal snagged its fur the last time the derrick was down, but that's not right, both the rabbits and foxes up here are white this time of year."

"They could have been caught in there from sometime in the Fall. I don't see how it could have anything to do with Danny's accident."

"It beats me," Luke replied and then went on, "I talked to the kid from town. He said he and George were out here the full time except for Christmas Day when he went home to have dinner with his family. He was pretty sure nobody came out during that time. However, when I questioned him a little further, he admitted they were drinking pretty heavy."

"It doesn't make sense. Danny would have rousted them up and at least had a drink with them."

"I agree. None of this makes any sense. By the way, have you heard from Kellie? She should be told about this."

"I have no idea where she is. I tried to contact her while I was in Calgary, but she was nowhere to be found."

The rig was ready to move the next morning. The trucks arrived at dawn, and everything was loaded up by noon. An old four-wheel-drive hearse came in and picked up the body with instructions to ship it to a funeral home in Edmonton. Luke hauled me out of a sound sleep after they had gone with some news. Two guys from Mid-Continent's Edmonton office took the news to Danny's widow. She went to pieces, but they were able to learn that Danny had been home for Christmas and the day after. He left on the 27th, telling his wife he had to meet a couple of co-workers for a ride back to the rig. That was the last she saw or heard from him.

I thought about this for a beat and then noticed the strange look on Luke's face.

"Are you thinking what I'm thinking?" I asked.

"Yeah, Kellie."

She didn't show up until two days after we had moved. The white Wagoneer pulled onto the lease just as we finished drilling surface hole. She stayed in her trailer the whole day, and it wasn't until the next morning that she came knocking at my door. One look at her face and I could tell she knew. She came in, hung her parka on the peg, and took a seat on the sofa. I didn't start in on her. I figured if she had something to tell me, she would eventually get it out.

It was her parka, which immediately caught my attention. I had seen it at least a dozen times before, but this was in a new context. The hood of the parka was fringed with the same fur, which I had found up by the monkey board. Suddenly a whole lot of questions were answered, and a larger bunch of new ones took their place.

"Do you want to tell me about it?"

"What do you mean?"

"What happened with you and Danny up on the monkey board?"

"It wasn't my fault," she sobbed. "He lost his footing. I was going to tell you. How did you know?"

I explained about the fur, and added, "Luke and I need to know the whole story. Are you willing to tell us everything?"

"Yes, but I am so scared of what will happen. Everyone will think it was my fault."

I went and got Luke.

"What's happening? I see your little buddy is back."

"You've got to come over and listen to this."

Kellie told her story, and as far as I could see, held nothing back. She and Danny had driven to Edmonton before Christmas. He went to spend the festive days with his family, and she booked into a hotel in the West Edmonton Mall. She picked him up on the 27th, and they stayed at the hotel until the 30th when they drove to Saskatchewan.

"One of Danny's many wild fantasies was to have sex up on the monkey board, but he could never talk his wife into it. We had been drinking, smoking some pot, and dropping acid for three days and were messed up pretty bad. We got to Amyot that evening. Danny kept bugging me all day to go up there with him and do it. Finally, I said, "Sure. What the hell" We drove out to the lease. As far as I could tell, there was no one here; at least I saw no lights. So, we climbed up the derrick. All I was wearing was that parka, and I was freezing my ass, but he kept yelling at me to keep climbing. He was really worked up when we got to the platform. He grabbed me and pushed me back against the edge. When he came at me, his feet slipped, and he went plunging past me over the railing. I grabbed him but couldn't hang on, and he fell. Even over the noise of the wind, I could hear him scream and the sound of his body hitting the ground."

She stopped, tried to control her sobbing then went on.

"I got down there as fast as I could. I think I slid halfway down the ladder. He was crumpled up on the ground barely moving, but he was still alive. The blood was flowing out of his neck. I tried to stop it, but it was coming too fast. He grabbed me and held on really tight, smiled at me, and then let go. At first, I could see his breath in the air and then nothing. I knew he was dead."

"What did you do then?"

"I ran over to the cooktent and George's trailer and banged on the door but couldn't raise anyone. I didn't know what to do. I panicked, took off, drove to town and booked into the hotel. The next morning I thought about going to the police and telling them what happened. Then I remembered what you two said about Constable Baker. So, I drove to Saskatoon and stayed at a hotel there."

Luke and I looked at each other. I had to believe we were thinking the same thing.

Finally, Luke asked her, "Who else have you told about this?"

"No one," she replied. "I haven't talked to anyone since it happened. I don't know what to do. I guess I thought no one would find out I was out here with him."

"Kellie, I think you had better go south and tell the whole story to your father, and let him decide what action to take. Luke and I need to talk."

"Okay. I'll get my stuff ready and see you before I go."

After she had gone, Luke observed, "That has to be about the craziest thing I've heard in a while, and no one would ever have known if you hadn't found that fur from her coat. I don't think she would have told us or anyone otherwise."

"I know. That came totally out of the blue. I was beginning to have visions of rabbits and foxes that had learned to climb ladders."

"Dusty, my gut tells me she's telling the truth. If it was anybody but those two, I'd be a bit suspicious, but Danny has always done crazy things ever since we've known him, and she's cut from the same cloth."

"So what do we do? Do we talk to the cops or bury it?"

"She was right not to go and see Charlie Baker. He would have screwed this up big time. I don't see a lot to be gained by making this a public spectacle. It was an accident, although the nature of the event was unique. Charlie Baker says it was an accident, so that should cover any other ideas people might have. Writing some fiction for the accident report will be a challenge, and explaining what he was doing fixing the monkey board in a snowstorm will be the ultimate test of my creative talents."

"Yes, that's something I definitely want to read. But another thing, Danny's wife is probably hurting enough without hearing all the actual details."

"So, we bury it," Luke observed.

"Something like that. It would appear to be our best choice, at least until we find out what Angleton is going to do. Maybe you should wait a few days before sending in your report."

A couple of days later, Martin Angleton called me. I got Luke on the line and we all agreed that we treat it as an accident and leave Kellie's name out of it. Kellie came back the next day, much more subdued than I had ever seen her.

"Thanks," was her only comment before she returned to her trailer.

A couple of days were spent in dealing with problems of lost circulation of the drilling mud in a very porous formation. A half a dozen batches of mud were mixed, each one thicker and containing more sawdust than the previous, and each batch disappeared into this low-pressure sand zone. Finally, the last mixture plugged the formation, and we were able to drill ahead.

Kellie wasn't much help. Consequently, I didn't get a lot of sleep over the next sixty-hour stretch. Finally, I had enough. I pounded on her trailer, told her to quit moping, and start processing the samples or go home. She agreed to take over. Since it was the weekend, I drove to Elena's to see her and get away from the noise of the rig. I debated with myself whether to tell her the truth about Danny's death. Finally, and again, I couldn't see any point in changing the story.

Two days with my lady more than made up for all the crap that had been coming down the previous week. Monday morning, I drove back and checked in at the doghouse for the morning report. As I was finishing up, Dozey came in off the rig floor.

"Did that fellow ever catch up with you?"

Dozey's words stumbled out slowly, as was the nature of his speech after the head accident he suffered five years previously.

"No, who was it?"

"Don't know. He never come over here."

"Did he talk to Luke?"

"Luke not here."

"What happened?" I asked, knowing it was going to take a while to get the whole story.

"We was pulling pipe, Lonnie working derrick. He yelled and pointed to your shack. White car there. Time I look again; it was gone."

"How long?"

"What?"

"How long was the car there?"

"Oh, uh, we pulled a couple more stands fore I looked again."

"What kind of car?"

"Don't know."

By now, I was getting frustrated, although I knew Dozey was doing his best. I had known him before the accident when he was one of the smartest young drillers in the oilpatch. He was on his way up the corporate ladder when a cable lowering the blocks had slipped and he had been hit. The blow put a significant dent in his hard hat as well as his head. A bunch of operations had put him back together with only a partial loss of speech and motor ability.

At this point, Lonnie came in off the floor to warm up. I asked him if he had a good look at the car and driver.

He thought for a minute and then said, "I saw it drive up and park by your trailer. This fellow got out, but I didn't get a look at his face. He was all bundled up. Anyway, he went into your trailer for probably ten minutes, and then he came out and drove away."

"You didn't recognize him?"

"No, like I told you, he had his face covered. He was about my height, five foot eight, but he was so bundled up I couldn't see much else."

"What about the car?"

"I'd know that one if I saw it again. It was a late sixties, white Chevy Suburban with a rusty dent on the driver's side rear panel."

"Thanks, I think I'd better go to town and see if I can find the car and who owns it. I don't like strangers in my trailer when I'm not there."

My search for the white Suburban was unsuccessful. I covered the few streets and alleys in town, drove up and down a few country roads, and even took runs over to the gas plant and up north to the mine.

Drilling was slow and uneventful over the next few days. On the weekend, I convinced Kellie to look after things, and Elena and I drove to Saskatoon. We spent a wonderful two days exploring this beautiful city. On Sunday evening, over a candlelight dinner, I asked Elena to marry me. It took her totally by surprise, and in fact, surprised me as well. I had not planned such a serious step, as I had vowed early in the game never to follow Shelly's path and never to get married so as to avoid all the commitments, responsibilities, and heartache involved. And now, I had jumped in with both feet after knowing this lady for such a short time.

"Dusty, are you sure of this? We've only been together for two months. I don't want you to commit to something you may regret later. I do love you and would answer yes, but I want us both to be sure."

Even though I was a bit disappointed, I knew she was right.

"Okay. Let's put it on hold until the end of your teaching term. I won't go out and buy the ring just yet."

"Thank you. It helps me with a decision I have to make. I am going to give the School Board notice that I will not be returning next September. I need to go work somewhere closer to civilized society. It will also give us time in the spring after you have gone on other jobs, and we have been apart, to see how we feel."

"I don't see me feeling any different."

"I don't either, but we need to be sure."

Monday morning, when I got back to the rig, drilling had stopped, and they were sitting on bottom, circulating. Big Tom was on shift, so I asked him, "What's going on?"

"Your girl wants a bottom-hole sample. She's worked up about something."

"You see anything?"

"Well, we got a drilling break, and there appears to be a bit of bubbling in the mud."

I checked the mud tank. There were some bubbles, but whether it was gas or just trapped air was difficult to tell.

As soon as I opened the trailer door, an excited Kellie pointed me toward the microscope.

"Take a look at this."

Even under low power, I could see the porous oil-stained sandstone.

"Looks good. How deep are you into it?"

"Only about three feet. Big Tom quit drilling as soon as he got the break in drill time, and I heard the gas detector go off. What do we do now?"

"Your call. What do you think we should do?"

"I think we should go in with the core barrel and cut a core."

"Okay, let's do it. Call the coring company and get them on their way. Tell them to call you when they are about three hours from here, so we don't have the drill string out of the hole too long. Have Tom keep circulating the mud until you give him the word, and have him add some weight material in case this is a high-pressure gas zone down there."

"What are you going to do? Are you going to take off again, and let me do all the work?"

"No, I'll stick around."

The fact was I was letting Kellie do it all as I thought it would help her get over Danny's death, and she did it well.

The core barrel arrived at midnight just as the last stand of drill pipe cleared the table. The bottom-hole samples looked very promising, and there was an oil-fluorescence on the surface of the mud in the tanks. We cut eighteen feet of easy coring on Tuesday and pulled it that evening. Kellie logged, labeled, and boxed the core. The roughnecks helped her with the heavy work. The girl was doing a good job. Her only question to me was whether we should run back in and take a second core.

"You've got to ask yourself if we are still in the sandstone, and is there any evidence that it contains saltwater?"

She thought for a minute and replied, "We are definitely still in the zone, but the sand doesn't look to be as porous, and the coring slowed down over the last few feet. How do you tell if it's wet?"

"Do a silver nitrate test. There's a bottle in my wellsite box. Pour a strip of silver nitrate solution along the bottom five feet of the core, and tell me what you see."

I watched as she carefully poured a stream of the clear fluid along the core. It showed no visible change.

"Nothing."

"Okay. If the core contained saltwater, it would react with the silver nitrate to form silver chloride, which would show up as a white powder on the core surface. Since you got nothing, it's probably not wet."

"So, we go back in and core some more," she concluded.

"One more thing. You want to be sure the sand is still porous, so take some chips from the bottom foot, and check them out under the microscope."

"The holes are still there, but they are smaller, and there are not as many. I still think we should cut some more core."

By Wednesday morning, the crew had finished reconditioning the hole and pulled out to put the core barrel back in. They were back on bottom by early afternoon.

According to the coring times and the cuttings, we broke out of the porous sandstone after drilling another six feet. To be sure we didn't get back into it; I watched it grind away at forty minutes a foot for a couple of hours. With nothing pressing to do, I decided to go in and spend the evening with Elena. I told Vince to cut another five feet and then pull out unless the drilling speeded up again.

I was at Elena's when her phone rang. She answered it and handed it to me.

"Dusty, it's Kellie. We got a two-foot break down to five minutes a foot. Now it's back again to slow drilling."

"Any gas kick from this little sand stringer?"

"No, nothing."

"Okay, cut another couple of feet and pull it. I'll be out there in about an hour."

I left Elena's around eight. She walked me to the truck and kissed me.

"I love you, Dusty, and will marry you."

It was the last time I saw her alive.

16

The core barrel was out of the hole by dawn. It had been a slow pull due to caving from the upper zones. Except for the top foot and a half, the sandstone from the second core was either wet or tight. By noon we were finished packaging it to be sent out for analysis. I had decided to test the top twenty feet and had Kellie phone the testing company to set it up while Dozey ran the drill string back in the hole to clean it.

I was in my trailer writing the final log and report when the two police cars pulled onto the lease. I was getting up to go over to see what was going on when Luke came and knocked on my door.

"Dusty, you need to come over and talk to these cops."

As I stepped out, I immediately recognized Charlie Baker, who was accompanied by a female officer, who even from this distance, looked familiar. As I approached them, I recognized Corporal Lucie Hansen. I immediately had a bad feeling about this.

It was Luke who spoke first, "Dusty, I don't know any other way to tell you this. Elena's body was discovered in her trailer this morning. The police tell me she was murdered."

"We need to ask you some questions," Lucie Hansen added. "We understand you, and she were very close."

Her lips were moving, but no sound was getting through. Elena was dead? It couldn't be. We were together yesterday. She agreed to marry me. There must be some mistake.

Luke was shaking me. I was lying on the ground but couldn't remember how I got there. Slowly I got to my feet and leaned unsteadily against the truck.

"Come into my shack and sit down. We'll talk in there. You need a drink."

I stumbled behind them into the trailer, still not too sure what was going on. I wouldn't believe that Elena was dead. It had to be a mistake. I was suddenly so very tired, but I could sense feelings of anger taking over. What kind of a cruel joke was this?

"How about telling me what happened," I responded.

I was getting madder by the minute.

Luke grabbed me firmly by the shoulders.

"Take it easy."

I sat down on his sofa, leaned over, and took a few deep breaths. He handed me a tumbler of whiskey, and I downed half of it in one gulp. The shock of the alcohol hit me and brought me back to reality. I took another drink, and a few more deep breaths then sat up.

Lucie Hansen took a long hard look at me.

"Do you want to hear this?"

I nodded, and she began, "When Elena Padrona
didn't show up for work at the school this morning,
they phoned her home. They received no answer, so
they called her landlord, Mrs. Stacker. She went
over to the trailer and found the body."

Slowly I assimilated the reality. There was no
doubt. The lady I loved was dead.

"How did she die?"

"Are you sure you want to get into this now?"
Luke questioned.

"I have to Luke. I loved her. We were going to
get married."

Reluctantly, Corporal Hansen went on, "She
was raped and then killed with a single bullet to the
back of the head from close range."

The shock hit me again. The brutality of the act
was more than I could wrap my mind around. I was
quiet for a few moments then asked, "Do you have
any idea who did it?"

"No, we have no suspects as yet. The Lab
people will be up this afternoon to go over the
place. We're hoping they can pick up some
fingerprints or other evidence, which could lead us
to the killer. We also thought you might have some
ideas as to who might be a suspect. When did you
last see her?"

"Yesterday evening. I have no idea who to
suspect. She had no enemies as far as I know."

"What time were you with her?"

"I left around eight. She walked me out to the
truck."

"Okay, that fits with the statement from her
neighbors."

"You mean the Stackers, her landlords?"

"No, the neighbors on the other side. The
Stackers were evidently not home at the time."

"I'd like to see her."

"Are you sure?" Lucie asked. "It's pretty bad."

"I have to."

"Okay, we've got some more questions. We might as well do it in town. You can follow us in."

Corporal Lucie Hansen's description of 'pretty bad' was an extreme understatement. It was horrible. My first reaction was to lose the contents of my stomach on the front lawn. There was blood everywhere. Elena's body was stretched out, face down, with the filmy nightgown I had given her for Christmas pulled up over her shoulders. Her beautiful raven hair was bunched up and soaked with blood at the back of her head. Blood had flowed beneath her body, sticking it to the floor.

Lucie Hansen stood close, ready to grab me if I passed out.

"The Medical Examiner flew up from Saskatoon this morning and has completed his work. We've had someone from our detachment in Edmonton notify her parents. As soon as the Lab people are finished, we will ship her body down there for services and burial."

"Can you turn her over?"

"I'd rather not, Dusty. Her face was totally blown away. You don't need that image in your memories of her. Let's go down to Charlie's office and fill out a statement."

"Does that mean I'm a suspect?"

"Everybody and nobody is a suspect," Lucie replied. "At present, we have nothing. We're hoping you can round out the picture we're building of her life in Amyot."

"I'll do what I can. I want to help you catch her killer."

Charlie Baker's office was one room on the

main floor of the town hall. The windowed wooden door opened into a counter, extending most of the length of the room. Behind it was a dented metal desk of indeterminate age and a wooden swivel chair doing its best to complete the destruction of the underlying threadbare rug. A couple of wanted posters, a fading picture of a younger Queen and a large calendar still sporting last month's page, adorned the walls. Charlie Baker had driven in ahead of us and was sitting with his feet up on the desk when we walked in. Quickly he planted them on the floor and tried to look officious.

"Relax, Charlie," Lucie said.

Charlie got up and offered her the seat of honor and then went and dug a folding chair out of the closet for me.

"I think I'll go home if you don't need me," he announced. He showed no concern about the events of the day.

"Sure, go ahead," Lucie replied. "I'll finish up with Dusty's statement."

When Charlie had shuffled out, she turned to me and said, "He doesn't like you very much. Can you tell me why?"

I gave her the official version of Danny's accident and how Luke and I made fun of him because he wouldn't go up the derrick to check it out.

"Would you have gone up?"

"I did and had a good look. We were probably a bit rough on him. He could have a problem with heights."

I went on to tell her about those friends of Elena's whom I knew, the difficult situation with her family and her previous relationship with Tom Morgan.

"Can you see Morgan as a suspect?"

I thought about it for a minute then replied, "No, I doubt it. He was somewhat unhappy about their breakup originally, but I sensed he was over it. He doesn't strike me as being the kind of person that would be able to do a thing like this, no matter how hurt or angry he was."

"Okay, I'll check him out and get back to you if I have any more questions. Don't go too far away."

"Where would I go? I've got a job to finish here. Anyway, I'm not leaving until we find her murderer."

I sensed she was not totally convinced of my innocence, and I guess I couldn't blame her. If I were a stranger to her, no doubt, I would have been the prime suspect.

When I got back to the trailer, Kellie was seated on the sofa.

"What…," I started, but she put her fingers to her lips.

"Shh," she voiced, and came over and put her arms around me and hugged me tightly. I could see her eyes were wet, and it was too much. I finally let my grief come out and buried my head on her shoulder

17

We were all set up to test the oil zone at dawn.
I had tried to call Dave several times, but there was
no answer. Finally, I contacted Millie's office and
left a message for her to relay to him. The test was a
success. We set the packers to expand above and
below the sand zone, thereby isolating it so that we
could be sure any fluid or gas recovered came from
the indicated oil horizon. With the tool open, we got
gas flowing to the surface almost immediately. It
blew steadily for an hour. When we pulled the pipe,
we found it half full of medium-grade crude oil with
no saltwater. The pressures weren't particularly
impressive, but there was no obvious drawdown.
With still no word from Dave, I decided to suspend
drilling. The hole had to be cleaned out, and I
figured I would wait a day to get some further
orders from Calgary. There was nothing more for
me to do right away.

That evening I drove into Meadow Lake and
phoned Elena's family. Her father was cordial but
very reserved. I could sense his sorrow over the
phone. The funeral was in two days. I phoned

Kellie, asked her to take over, and left for Edmonton. I stayed overnight in North Battleford. The next morning I ordered flowers to be sent to Carl Padrona's church and had myself fitted for a new suit. I was doing okay until the realization struck me that this could have been the suit I would have been wearing at my wedding. That evening I booked into an Edmonton motel. Depression was taking over as the new reality captured my mind. The total sadness of knowing I would never be able to be with her or hold her again was too much.

The closed casket service was held in Big Carl's church. His eulogy was beautiful, and I could physically feel the pain the man was suffering. Next came Carl Junior. I had to get up and leave when he started his usual fire and brimstone routine. I was not alone, as Ginny and a few other family members and friends were not prepared to listen to his ravings. Their house was filled for the reception. The only folks I had met were her immediate family, and I felt uncomfortable and very much an outsider, but I guess from their point of view, I was. I made my way methodically around the room, mouthing the expected words of condolences to the individual members of her family. Only her mother responded and made any effort to share her feelings.

"Elena loved you very much. I felt when she left that the two of you would be happy together. My first reaction to the tragedy was to blame you for coming into her life. Now I feel maybe God didn't bless your union and chose to take her from us."

That told me it was time to go. As I walked out the door, Ginny stepped in beside me and said, "I want to apologize for my family and their 'holier than thou' attitude. Always remember that you were the best thing that ever happened to Elena."

She gave me a hug and walked back into the house.

As I drove out of the city, the reality of the past few days finally hit me full force. The total loneliness and absolute and utter sadness I felt forced me to pull into a rest stop until I got my emotions under control. I picked up a six-pack and finished it by the time I hit Grande Centre, where common sense finally prevailed, and I realized this was not making the pain go away, and I was too drunk to drive any farther. I checked into the hotel, had dinner, and went to bed.

Sleep was elusive and difficult to retain when I finally did drop off. The night was a kaleidoscope of dreams and periods of painful reality. She was in all the dreams, beautiful, vibrant, and just out of reach. When I tried to approach, the image dissolved into nothingness. She was there with me in the past and in places we planned for the future. Our whole life together, which might have been, was condensed into a series of one-act plays.

In the morning, I felt like hell. It was like I hadn't gone to bed. I usually don't remember my dreams, or they are fleeting images that fade with the morning light. But last night's were still vivid, piercing my conscious fog like the lights of an oncoming car.

I needed a drink. No, that's not right. I wanted a drink or two, or maybe many. And so went the day. I paid for another night and had drunk myself into a stupor by day's end.

That night, Elena was back. This time the picture was hazy and disjointed. I reached for her, and she became someone else. Some images were familiar; others were strangers. I awoke with a start when the last vision became a faceless man with a gun. I tried to focus on his face in a half-awake state, but it was a blur. Sleep was impossible after that.

I got up, walked around a bit, and then had a hot bath. Finally, I fell into a dreamless sleep until some idiot kept honking his horn in the parking lot outside my window. It was dinnertime. I had slept the day away. A long walk around the little town in the cold, my first decent meal in two days, and I was ready for bed again.

It has been written that there are certain instances or events in life, which, when looked back upon, define a significant element or period of change. It is the point in the journey when you cease to be what you were and begin to be what you are to become. When I awoke the next morning, I somehow felt I was entering one of these periods. Getting ready to shave, my first look in the mirror was a shock. An old man was staring back at me, complete with graying hair and wrinkles. Suddenly, my image of enduring youth was gone, along with any claims I might have to immortality. I fully expected Shelly's voice to come through with an 'I told you so.' What was left? Where do I go from here, and did any of it really matter? I had lost the only thing that had any meaning, the lady I loved. At least the next step was vividly clear. I had to find the person that took her away and see to his destruction.

Heading back to the well, I felt relaxed for the first time since Elena's death. I was just west of Meadow Lake, when my mobile phone rang, activating the horn. Now I knew who the idiot was whose horn had awakened me the day before. The call was from Millie, and she sounded a bit frantic.

"Dusty, we've got a big-time problem. Dave Stenowicz is almost two months behind in paying our invoices. I've been phoning every day for the past week, but there's been no reply, so yesterday I went over there. The office is empty and closed up. When I called his wife, she said she has no idea where he is. They are going through a divorce; all communication is through the lawyers. I don't know what else I can do. I know you've been through a really tough time, but I think you should handle it from here."

I thought for a moment and then replied, "I'll try and deal directly with Angleton. He's the one financing this thing, so it's in his best interest to see it to completion, especially since this last hole looks like a winner. Just let me look after it from here."

"I would appreciate that, but are you sure you're up to dealing with it? Your little girl up there told me what happened to Elena. Dusty, I feel so sad for you. I know what you're going through. When Tony was killed, I didn't care if I lived or died, except for our son."

This news about Dave's disappearance, which a week ago would have sent me into fits of anxiety and worry, now didn't strike me as particularly important or relevant to my life. I guess on some subconscious level; I expected it to happen.

I reached Amyot in mid-afternoon and headed for the police office. Fortunately, I caught up with Lucie Hansen just as she was set to leave for Meadow Lake.

"Are you getting anywhere with the investigation?"

"Maybe. I don't know if it means anything. I understand you had a run-in a while back with this fellow they call Moose. Mr. Stacker described him as a squawman from the Reserve north of here. Mr. Stacker said you banged him up pretty bad."

"Yeah, we had a scuffle in the bar when I first got up here, but what's that got to do with the murder?"

"I'm just considering the possibility that he might have wanted to get to you by killing her. You are evidently not that popular among the locals."

"C'mon Lucie, that's a bit of a stretch."

"That's true, but someone did see Elena getting out of his truck in front of her place earlier that afternoon."

"That is odd. She did kind of play a part in the bar fight. In fact, that's where I met her, but I can't see him killing her for revenge. He would have just come out to the rig and shot me. Who saw her get out of his truck?"

"The Branyons, the neighbors next door."

I went on to recount the events of that evening and how Elena sticking her foot out at the right time probably saved me from being taken down.

"Have you talked to Moose?" I asked.

"I can't find him. Constable Baker went up to the Reserve where Moose lives, but his wife said he was out on his trap line. I guess we'll have to wait for him to come in. I have one other question. Do you own a gun?"

"I've got a .45 Magnum. It's in my trailer at the wellsite."

"Would you bring it in with a couple of shells? I want to check it out against the shell casing we found in the trailer."

"That answers my next question. I guess I'm still a suspect."

"As far as I'm concerned, anyone who ever had contact with her is suspect, along with the possibility it was a random act by someone passing through. I can't rule out anyone."

At that point, it was evident to me she was the only one investigating, and she wasn't making much headway.

As I drove onto the lease, I observed the pumps were running to keep the mud circulating in the hole, but no one was in the doghouse or on the rig floor. Luke came out of his trailer as I drove in and motioned me over.

"We need to talk," he said. "I had to turn the crews loose. Orders came down yesterday from head office to shut things down until further notice. Evidently, they haven't been paid in over a month, and they can't locate this fellow Stenowicz to find out what's going on. The word is I'm to sit and circulate until I hear different."

"I need to talk to Kellie and get her to tell her father to loosen the purse strings and put this show back on the road."

"I'm afraid she took off as soon as I told her about the shutdown. She didn't say where she was going or when she was coming back."

"Yeah, that sounds like Kellie. Let's hope she has gone to stir her old man into action."

Kellie returned the evening of the next day. She immediately asked Luke and me to come over to her trailer. When we entered, a distinguished older gentleman greeted us warmly.

"Martin Angleton," he introduced himself. "Kellie has told me much about you two gentlemen. It's my pleasure to meet you finally."

We shook hands and seated ourselves around the small living area. I estimated Angleton to be in his mid or late sixties, although he carried himself like a younger man. He had a full head of snow-white hair, worn long, almost to his collar. He was tall, probably six-two or three, with a lean frame carrying little fat. Most notable were his hands. Long fingers like those of a pianist were perfectly manicured. His clothing was an outfit often seen in the Calgary boardrooms, an eastern banker trying to fit into the western scene with the typical attire of a wannabe cowboy, complete with leather boots and fitted jeans. I looked around for the usual cowboy hat. His greeting seemed warm and genuine, but the voices in my head were telling me to be very careful in my dealings with this man.

"As you probably know by now, Mr. David Stenowicz of Stenowicz Oilfield Services has disappeared. My investigations have discovered he has fled with a substantial amount of cash to an as yet unknown South American country, probably Brazil. I've also learned he has attempted to transfer funds, forwarded to him for this project, to some offshore accounts. However, that is my problem, which is well on the way to being solved. Your concerns, as I perceive them, are regarding the sums of money needed to wind this project up successfully. Luke, I have arranged for Mid-Continent to be paid. You will be informed in the morning when they receive my cheque, to resume operations. Dusty, your invoices are being taken care of, as are those of all the suppliers and contractors holding outstanding accounts. My hope is that we can minimize this interruption and complete the job. I will be flying back to Calgary in the morning to finish clearing this up. Kellie will keep me apprised of the operation on a daily basis."

"There are a couple of things we need to decide before we proceed," I replied. "The first one is easy. What do you want to do with this well? It has the potential for limited oil production and will probably pay itself out, but that would require further treatment and testing. Alternatively, which is what I would suggest, we can cap it and do the production tests at a later date. The second question involves the upcoming land sale. Stenowicz indicated to me he had posted the land, and this program was designed to gather the data necessary to determine a meaningful bid. I don't know if that is true or not. You need to find out if he did post the land. Based on what we've learned from this well, for which, hopefully, only we know the results, the area has potential, and a meaningful bid should be determined."

"I've seen the posting," Angleton replied. "Mr. Stenowicz was quite insistent; I was aware he had taken that step. As far as calculating a bid, I have no idea how to proceed. Is it something you could do?"

"I can, but it's not my area of competence. I would sooner have you contract it out to a colleague of mine, Jeremy Prince, who certainly has more expertise than I. Kellie knows Jeremy. He was one of her instructors at SAIT. Time is of the essence, as I think the sale is coming up soon."

"That sounds reasonable," Angleton observed. "Would you contact Mr. Prince and give him the information he will need. He can get in touch with me for terms of his employment."

Kellie drove her father to Meadow Lake the next morning to take his charter south. I was waiting for her when she returned.

"Tell me if what I heard between the lines last night is correct."

"Okay."

"Stenowicz tried to ship all the money earmarked for this project to his accounts offshore."

"He tried," she replied, "but it was not completely successful. My father is a personal friend of the manager of Stenowicz's bank, so when the first transfers went through, he let us know. Consequently, Dad put some claim on the rest of the funds as well as Stenowicz's personal and business accounts. So far as we can tell, he and his little secretary went south with about two hundred grand, but the rest of his money is all tied up."

It was snowing again as we walked over to the cook tent. The temperature, which had been hovering in the twenty below range for the past week, had now moderated to zero with the arrival of the new storm. Big George was in the middle of unpacking all the gear he had boxed when he heard the money had run out. He was not in a good mood.

"I hear we're back in business for a few days," was his curt greeting.

Fortunately, the coffee was warmer than George's hello. Kellie and I sat down with a couple of cups.

"Kellie, there's something I have to tell you about the last hole. Do you remember you questioned why we were drilling so much granite?"

"I know," she said. "I saw the gold."

"Where?"

"There were fines in some of the stuff, which went through the shaker screen. I guess you missed scooping that up. I didn't know if you were going to tell me about it or not. You must have thought me pretty stupid not to figure that one out."

"No, I just thought you had enough other things on your mind and wouldn't catch on."

"Were you ever going to tell me?"

"I just did."

"No, I mean if the situation here hadn't

changed."

"I don't know. At that point, I was concerned about not getting paid. If this financial thing hadn't been resolved, I probably wouldn't have told you. At least, I would have been able to walk away from this fiasco with something."

She thought for a minute and then said, "I guess I probably would have done the same thing."

By morning the storm had blown itself out, leaving another blanket of white to cover man's feeble efforts. After getting the go-ahead from Mid-Continent, Luke had spent the last eighteen hours trying to reassemble his crews. Many of them had gone home and could see no point in coming back for a few days work. He decided to go with two twelve-hour shifts instead of three eights. Dozey was the only driller to return, so Luke had to do one of the shifts himself. We had decided to run the production string and cap the well, leaving further testing for later. Because of the delay, it was going to take a couple of days to get the production pipe and wellhead delivered.

The initial investigations into Elena's death had turned up no leads, at least any that I was being told about. Lucie Hansen had returned to Saskatoon, and as far as I could tell, Charlie Baker just sat around his office with his feet on the desk doing very little. I was getting the feeling there was an official loss of interest creeping in, and if any progress was going to be made, it would be up to me. The trouble was I didn't know where to start. The police had sealed the trailer, leaving everything unchanged. The Lab people had driven up and checked it out. Either they had found nothing meaningful, or Lucie wasn't going to tell me if they had. After all, she still considered me a suspect.

It was late afternoon when I went into town. I drove by the trailer and was about to continue when I noticed a light on in the house next door. On an impulse, I decided to stop and have a talk with these folks that had seen Elena getting out of Moose's truck. They were cordial, invited me in, and sympathized with my loss. They were an older couple. I guessed them to be in their early seventies. The Branyons had lived in Amyot since Mr. Branyon had an accident at the mine, which had left him partially paralyzed and confined to a wheelchair.

"I get sick of watching TV, so I spend a lot of time looking out the window watching our little world go by. That's how I happened to see Miss Padrona get out of that truck. I knew it wasn't yours. We'd gotten real familiar with seeing you parked out there," he chuckled.

"Did you see who was driving?"

"Yes, sir, a big fellow. He had long hair below his toque and a beard. The woman with him was short and plump."

"He had a woman with him?"

"That's right, and a boy. I'd say the boy was about ten or eleven. That truck cab was sure packed with the four of them. When Miss Padrona got out, she stopped by the driver's door, and they talked for a few minutes before she went to her trailer, and the truck drove off."

"Did you know Elena very well?"

Mrs. Branyon, a tall, sharp-featured but attractive lady, replied, "We would always wave to each other and stop and chat when we met. She came over a couple of times to help me with my house cleaning. She was a lovely girl. It was such a tragedy."

I thanked them when I realized they had no more information to offer.

As I stepped down from the Branyon's porch, I noticed the light was now on at Barty's.

According to Lucie, they hadn't been home when Elena was killed, but I thought it wouldn't hurt to stop in and have a talk. Maybe something might have occurred to them since they had answered her questions.

Only Anna Lea and their kids were home when I knocked. She was in the process of trying to put the four of them to bed. She invited me in and set me down in the kitchen with a coffee while she tried to corral the four wild little creatures. It put me in mind of a lion tamer trying to collect his animals after a circus act. All that was missing was the chair and the whip. After half an hour of bedlam, she motioned me into the living room, where she flopped down into a big upholstered recliner that occupied the corner across from a television. A well-worn patterned sofa ran along the sidewall, and a couple of occasional chairs occupied the other side. A large burl coffee table in the center of the room partially hid the threadbare carpet. It was a well lived-in room. Dime store hunting pictures adorned three of the walls. The fourth wall, behind the recliner, sported the heads of a moose and what looked like a trophy bighorn sheep.

The last and only time I had talked to Anna Lea was the night of the bar fight. Although all my attention had been focused on Elena, I did have a mental image of Anna Lea as a mousy, but somewhat attractive, slim blonde woman with an air of sadness. Now, sitting across from me was an older version of that image attired in a formless print dress, with no make-up and touches of gray in her hair. Only the look of sadness had not changed.

"I'm sorry; Barty isn't home to meet with you. This is one of his poker nights with his friends, so there's no telling what time he'll be in."

I apologized for coming unannounced but went on to explain I was trying to get a feel for what happened the night of the murder.

"I don't know what I can tell you," she replied. Her voice was quiet, not soft, but monotone without expression. "We were out all evening. I was at my parents' place south of here with the kids. I left them with Mom overnight and got back here about midnight. I remember seeing no light on in the trailer, so I assumed Elena had gone to bed."

"So, you and Barty got back about midnight?"

"No, Barty had gone over to a friend's to work on a car. He got home earlier and went to bed. He was asleep when I got in."

"Neither of you saw or heard any signs of someone prowling around that evening?"

"No, and when Barty shoveled the walks the next morning, he didn't see any footprints in the snow. This surprised me since Elena was usually up early and had already walked to school by the time we ate breakfast, and he had gotten the shovel out."

"Didn't you think it was strange enough to check on her?"

"No. Barty had to head off to work, and I drove back to get the kids. I'm sorry I'm not more help. She was a wonderful friend, and I'll miss her. I hope they find who did this."

I thanked her and drove back to the well. She hadn't told me anything of consequence, but something she had said, or actually the way she had said it, was scratching away at my mind. When I pulled up to my trailer, it hit me. Everything Anna

Lea had voiced was totally without feeling. I
believed what she had told me, but it was puzzling
that she seemed to express no emotion over Elena's
death.

18

Things got active a couple of days later when
the production pipe arrived. It had to be measured
and calculated to the hole depth. Running the string
went like clockwork, and the cement truck arrived
just as we reached bottom. By the next morning, the
pipe had been cemented in place. It needed twenty-
four hours to set, so Kellie and I drove into town for
a decent breakfast. With most of the crews gone,
George's head wasn't into cooking, and the results
showed it. When we drove back onto the lease, an
old battered truck was idling in front of my trailer.
Immediately, I had a bad feeling about it. Luke was
on the rig floor but ran down the doghouse steps
waving his arms as we drove up.

"You've got company," he announced as I
opened the driver's side window. "I think it's that
fellow from the Reservation the cops are looking
for."

I took another look at the truck. It certainly fit
the description the Branyons had given Lucie
Hansen, a red, rusty old Ford F-100 with body
damage.

"Yeah, it's probably him."

I couldn't tell if Moose was alone.

"Kellie, you drive my truck over to your trailer. I don't want you nearby if there's any problem."

"Have you got your gun?" Luke asked.

"It's in my desk in the trailer, but it won't be of much help if he comes at me out here."

"Do you want me to get mine and walk with you?"

"No, I'm going to play it cool, go over and see what he wants. Unless he's drunk, I don't think he'll do anything."

As I walked across the lease area toward my trailer, the door to the truck opened, and Moose stepped out and stood by the front fender. From the other side, his wife appeared and walked toward me.

"My husband wants to talk to you," she said.

"Okay," I replied with interest. "We'll talk over in that tent where it's warmer."

I pointed to the cook tent. They climbed back into the truck and drove over and parked by the entrance. I knew I didn't want them in my trailer with me alone.

Kellie and George were in the cook tent when we came in. Kellie showed no inclination to leave, and I noticed she had a brown leather case beside her. George served up some coffee, and we sat down. Moose's wife, Della, did most of the talking. Mr. Branyon's description of her as short and plump was an understatement. She was as round as she was tall. Her thick black hair was cut short and crowned a moon-shaped face of broad flat features. I could see where she must have been quite attractive as a young woman, but a tough life on the Reserve had taken its toll.

"The police are looking for my husband. They

think he killed the schoolteacher. The policeman came to our home and demanded to know where he was. He said my husband was wanted for murder and would be arrested."

I could picture Charlie Baker going up to the Reserve and throwing his weight around with people who weren't going to give him any trouble.

I turned to Moose, "Did you kill Miss Padrona?"

Moose had been slouched over while his wife spoke. Now he straightened up and looked me straight in the eye.

"No. She was good teacher and help my son learn. I not kill her."

"So, he was home with you that evening?" I asked his wife.

"Yes, all evening, then we went to bed."

I knew they had to talk to the police, but not Charlie Baker. They needed to tell their story to Lucie. I believed them but knew Charlie Baker would probably arrest Moose anyway. I told them to wait while I tried to contact Lucie.

I phoned her number in Saskatoon but was informed that she had left for Amyot that morning. I called the Amyot office, and Charlie Baker answered. I identified myself and asked to speak to Corporal Hansen. Charlie informed me she was busy, and he would take whatever message I had.

I was starting to lose it with this jerk.

"Look Constable, or whatever you are; I suggest you pass the phone over to Corporal Hansen. This is important, and if I have to, I'll come down and give her the message in person. It pertains to Elena Padrona's murder. She will want to hear about it, and I suggest for your job security, you put her on the phone."

Charlie dropped the phone, picked it up, and I could hear the squeaking of his chair before Lucie's voice finally answered me.

"Boy, you really got him going this time," she started.

"I know, but that idiot keeps pissing me off every time I have to deal with him."

"Okay, he'll survive. What do you have to tell me?"

"I've got Moose and his wife out here at the rig. We've had a talk. I'm convinced he had nothing to do with Elena's death."

"Oh! I think they better come in and see me."

"That's what I told them. They'll only come if I go in with them. See if you can convince the Constable to go home before we get there. He's already threatened to put Moose in jail."

"Okay, I'll take care of it, and bring that gun of yours in when you come."

Moose and Della got in their truck and waited for me to follow while I went into the trailer to get the gun. I opened the bottom drawer, where I usually keep it locked in. The drawer wasn't locked, and my Magnum was missing.

"Your gun is missing? What do you mean, missing? Did you lose it? Was it stolen? What do you expect me to believe by all this? First, you keep stalling about bringing it in. Now you tell me it's gone."

Lucie Hansen was angry. Somehow, I didn't blame her. I probably would have had trouble believing my story if I was in her shoes. She had sent Charlie Baker home, as I requested, agreeing that the couple would not be comfortable in his presence. She had listened to their account of the events of that afternoon when they gave Elena a ride home, had them sign a statement, and sent them home. Then she started in on me.

"Lucie, I'm just telling you the way it is. The last time I saw the gun was the morning we were shot at. After we came down from the ridge, I put it in the drawer and thought I locked it, but maybe I didn't. Things were a bit exciting that day. I have no idea what happened to it."

We looked at each other in silence for a few minutes, and then she said, "Dusty, I'm trying to believe you had nothing to do with her death, but at times like this, it's difficult. Did you bring any of the shells, so we could compare them with the casing we found?"

"No, the shells went missing as well. They were with the gun."

"Well, I guess I'm back to where I started with no obvious suspect and a town full of possibles."

The next morning the cement was set on the production casing, and I released the rig. It would take two or three days for Luke and the remaining crew to get everything torn down and loaded onto trucks to be taken to the next well or a storage yard. We would bring a service company in to set the well up for production. They would install the wellhead and shut it in until production tests were run. Except for reports and forms to fill out, my work was done. They moved my trailer out with the rig.

For a moment, I had considered going home to get away from this deep freeze, but I knew I had to stay in Amyot. I needed to see Elena's killer caught. Lucie Hansen had suggested I stay nearby while the investigation was ongoing. I was still a suspect. Finding the murderer was the only way I would be able to clear my name and satisfy my need for vengeance.

I put all the paperwork in a rough form and asked Kellie to deliver it to Millie for the final processing. We also worked out a plan for staking a substantial claim block to cover the potential gold-bearing area. Kellie was hooked up to her trailer and gone before the rig left the lease. I drove to town and booked a room in the Amyot Hotel, paying a week in advance.

The Amyot Hotel was a bit of a misnomer. It was, in reality, a moneymaking bar supporting a few rooms for rent on the second floor. As evidenced by my room, which supposedly was the best one, most of the profits went back into the bar and the owners' pockets. My home for the week had the bare essentials. The bed was of indeterminate age with a mattress, which had a permanently adjusted shape to accommodate the bulk of its heavier inhabitants. There was a sink with running cold and sometimes warm water. For the luxury of any other bathroom functions, one had to venture down to the end of the hall. This special place served all of the eight sleeping rooms. I could easily imagine the chaos when the place was fully occupied, and everybody wanted a morning shower. Fortunately, I was the only occupant. An overstuffed chair of a faded floral design, a wall mirror, and a couple of dusty reproductions of cowboy scenes completed the décor. After one night, I longed for the comfort of my apartment.

To my mind, the investigation was going nowhere, and I was at a loss as to what meaningful action I could take. Lucie Hansen had returned to Saskatoon, but before she left, the Branyons had called her to assure themselves they had not jeopardized her work by talking to me. At first,

Lucie told me to stay out of the investigation and let the police do their job, but after further discussion, I assured her I just wanted to talk to a few of the town folk, and I would pass on to her anything I learned.

"And besides, I don't see Charlie Baker playing much of a role in this search."

For most of the week, I walked around the village, spending time in some of the spots where people gathered. I got a haircut and chatted with the boys that hung around the barbershop. I used the same approach at the general store, where I picked up a few things I didn't need. Evenings were spent in the hotel bar.

On Thursday morning, I went to the bank to clean out my local account. I had decided to pull out of Amyot Sunday morning and head south. The young lady teller who waited on me looked somewhat familiar. It wasn't until she reminded me we had met briefly at Elena's curling match that I remembered her, a slightly overweight redhead, who had been throwing the lead rocks for the bank's team.

"It was really sad for me to learn about Elena. I felt we had grown to be friends over the few months that I knew her. I can't believe she's gone. You know, she dated my cousin Tom a few times before she met you. In fact, I introduced them."

"You mean Tom Morgan is your cousin?"

"That's right. Tom was interested in meeting her when she first arrived, but this other fellow kept asking Elena for a date. She didn't want to go out with him, so she went to a couple of dances with Tom. I somehow felt she might have been using Tom to discourage the other guy."

"Do you know who this other man was?"

"Sure, it was the cop, Baker."

So, Charlie Baker had tried to date Elena back in September, and she had turned him down. I couldn't help wondering why that little bit of information hadn't come out before. Rather than confront the Constable right away, I decided to talk to Tom first. I called him at the gas plant and was able to reach him on his lunch break. I invited him to meet me for a beer after work.

"Yes, that's right. Molly introduced us. Elena asked me to take her to the dance to get Charlie Baker to quit chasing her. It worked. She told me he quit calling her right after that. Trouble was I was starting to fall for her when you showed up."

"You mean Charlie gave up after your first date with her?"

"That's what she told me," he replied. "She said he would completely ignore her whenever they met somewhere afterward."

I thanked Tom, and after he left, sat for a while, pondering the significance of this new information and what to do with it. I had assured Lucie Hansen I would call her if I learned anything new. This certainly qualified in the something new category, so I put in the call.

Corporal Lucie Hansen drove up to Amyot the next morning. I was finishing my breakfast in the hotel café when she walked in and sat down in the booth across from me.

"Okay, tell me the story."

So I did.

"Are you sure you're not trying to put Constable Baker under suspicion because you don't like him?"

"Look, Corporal," I replied angrily, "I am just telling you what Tom Morgan and his cousin told me. Granted, I think the Constable is an asshole, but that doesn't color what I am saying to you. You should go and talk to them yourself if you don't believe me."

"Oh, I plan to, and we'll see what Constable Baker has to say as well."

"Why don't you interview him first and see if he lies to you about ever knowing her."

I knew I had pushed it too far when she didn't answer and promptly got up from the table and left.

I didn't hear from Lucie again until the next day. I was getting ready to leave the room when she knocked on the door. I invited her down for breakfast.

When we were seated, she said, "I was angry as hell at you when I stomped out of here yesterday. Then I got thinking maybe you might be right. I talked to Molly at the bank, and she confirmed what you told me."

"What about Charlie Baker?"

"That's internal police information. I can't discuss it with you."

The look on her face told me Charlie had probably lied to her.

"So, if I hear anything else, who do I report to, you or Constable Baker?"

"You talk to me. I'm staying up here until this thing is resolved one way or another."

Then she added, "Besides, Constable Baker is on temporary leave."

It was encouraging for me to hear Lucie Hansen was going to devote all her efforts toward the investigation, but discouraging to realize that no real progress was being made. It was Saturday, and I could see no point in remaining in Amyot any longer. When I told Corporal Hansen I was leaving on Sunday, she agreed and promised to let me know if there were any new developments.

Saturday afternoon, I packed up, which took all of twenty minutes. I dropped into the bar that evening for what I figured would be my last Amyot beer. By nine o'clock, the place was packed with the usual crowd of serious drinkers and the more adventurous couples shuffling around the dance floor. By the second beer, it didn't seem like such a good idea, revisiting the scene of my first evening with Elena. By the fourth or fifth beer, it was beginning to feel like a better idea. I didn't realize until then how many people I had met during the past week that sympathized with my loss. Half the village seemed to stop by my table and offer to buy me a drink. Just before midnight, a young fellow who looked vaguely familiar sat down at my table. As I was delving into the fog to put a name with the face, he said, "I saw that white Suburban again yesterday."

That kicked in my memory. It was Lonnie, Dozey's derrickman, who had replaced Danny, and who had seen the car pull up by my trailer that day.

By now, I wasn't in too good a shape to understand much, but through my alcoholic haze, I could make out that Lonnie, who lived in Meadow Lake, had seen the white Chevy Suburban parked in some bushes near a house south of Amyot. He recognized it from the driver's side dent. Fortunately, he was sober and quickly realized that I wasn't, so he drew me a map of the car's location. He also included his phone number in case the whole thing was a mystery to me in the morning.

"It's kinda hard to see from the road," he said. "You have to be looking in the right direction from the right spot."

Later that evening, someone got me upstairs

and poured me into bed. I never did find out for sure who it was to thank them.

Sunday morning dawned bright, sunny, and cold. Even with the best of intent, I was in no condition to search for any white cars. Being Sunday, the hotel café was closed, and the streets were deserted. Last night's partiers were either sleeping it off or atoning for their sins at the local church. I had no choice but to drive to the Husky truck stop if I was to get anything to eat. My truck had been sitting in the hotel parking lot for the week, not plugged in, and of course, wouldn't start. This left me with the choices of either going back to bed hungry or trudging down to the Husky restaurant. Hunger won out. At least the cold walk cleared my head. The boys at the station agreed to come and get the truck, thaw it out and charge the battery. The rest of the day was a total loss.

19

On Monday morning, I paid for two more days stay and decided to go hunting for the white Suburban. A snowfall during the night had covered everything, creating a village wonderland. I had reentered the human race far enough to appreciate the beauty and be concerned that spotting the van under these conditions was going to be a challenge. I considered calling Lonnie, but on second thought decided I'd give it a try myself. I retrieved my truck from the Husky station and headed south.

According to Lonnie's map, which I finally discovered crumpled up in the pocket of my jeans, the Chevy was parked in a grove of trees in a field just to the south of a small farmhouse about eight to ten miles from Amyot. His map gave no descriptions as to the appearance of the home or any additional information. Fortunately, there were few homesteads along this stretch of road. I spotted the setting that fit the description just past the eleven-mile mark. A recently-plowed lane led up to a small frame house, badly in need of paint, set well back from the road. A barbed-wire fence separated it from a pasture, which was also served by a lane entrance. On the pasture side of the fence, just past the house, was a group of spruce trees of equal size set out in a pattern, probably the result of someone's effort to grow marketable Christmas trees. I could see no signs of the Suburban. I drove back and forth a few times, trying to observe this little forest from different angles, as Lonnie had suggested. Finally, in desperation, I parked the truck at the field entrance, climbed over the locked gate and trudged my way through the snow toward the trees. I was about thirty feet from the edge of the grove when I spotted it, the white Chevy Suburban with a large dent in the back left panel, just as Lonnie had described it. As I suspected, the blanket of snow obscured it from the road. I walked around the vehicle and eventually spotted three bullet holes. All my shots had found their mark. There was no doubt this was the same vehicle George, and I had seen up on the ridge.

It was locked. I tried all the doors, but there was no access. I remembered that I had put the diagram I had made of the tire tracks on the ridge in my wallet. I dug it out, and although I knew it was the same truck, I compared it to the tread pattern on this vehicle. They were a perfect match. The tires were a popular Firestone series, which probably supported half the cars in the area, so it didn't really prove anything. In this case, it didn't matter. I copied the license plate number with the hope of identifying the registered owner.

On impulse, I looked up toward the house and caught the slight movement of a curtain in the nearest window. I thought I saw someone there, but I couldn't be sure. I decided to pay the folks at the house a visit.

As I climbed through the fence, I looked up

again quickly and spotted an elderly man standing behind the window. He moved away immediately and closed the curtains. A small covered porch led to the back door. My knocking brought only the muffled barking of a dog. There was no human acknowledgment of my presence. After a couple of minutes, I rapped again. Nothing. The same scenario repeated itself at the front door. Either these folks had a fear of strangers, a serious need for hearing aids, or something to hide. I walked the plowed lane back to the road. Their mailbox sat at the end of the lane. The inscribed name, J. P. Marshall, meant nothing. I was tempted to check out their mail but figured I had enough problems without getting in trouble with Canada Post.

On the way back to town, I reviewed what I had accomplished. I found the white Suburban, which had brought someone to shoot at me from the ridge and subsequently visit me at the wellsite. The Marshals probably owned it, or someone else had permission to park it there. In other words, I wasn't any wiser than I was before.

I needed answers to two questions. Who was the registered owner of the Suburban, and who were the Marshals? The first question would involve having Corporal Lucie Hansen doing a check with Motor Vehicles. I wasn't prepared to lay this one on Lucie and answer all her questions quite yet, as I was still probably on her suspect list. The problem of identifying the Marshals should be easier. The obvious person to ask, one who probably knew most of the folks in the area, was Tom Morgan's cousin, Molly, the bank teller.

It was a few minutes before closing time when I walked into the bank. An elderly couple was finishing up their business at Molly's wicket as I got in line.

"Hi," she greeted me cheerfully. "I thought you'd be gone from here by now."

"I know. That's what I had planned, but these little mysteries connected with Elena keep grabbing a hold of me."

"So, you're still trying to do the police's job, tracking down whoever killed her. I hope you get him. The lady cop was in and asked me a whole bunch of questions about Charlie Baker, but I didn't know anything more than what I told you. I got the feeling she didn't figure him for a suspect, but what would you expect, both being cops."

"I don't think he had anything to do with it, either."

"You're probably right, but what brings you in today? You withdrew all your money, and I doubt if my beauty has smitten you."

I smiled and said, "Don't be so sure of that, but I have another question for you. Do you know a J. P. Marshal?"

Molly thought for a minute, and then replied, "That would be Paul Marshal. I don't know him. He doesn't bank here, but I think he lives to the south, toward Meadow Lake. He probably does his banking business down there. I did know his son, Paul Junior. I went to high school with him, but he took off out of here right after graduation. I haven't seen him since. Paul had an older sister, and she's still around. I often see her in town, but she doesn't bank here either. Let see; her name is Ann, or Ann Marie, or something like that."

"Could it be Anna Lea?"

"Yes, that's it. She's married to some fellow that works at the gas plant with Tom and has a whole bunch of kids."

I thanked Molly and returned to the truck.
Finally, another piece clicked into place, but what
did it mean? The Suburban was parked at Anna
Lea's parent's home. I needed to know who the
owner was, and I wasn't quite ready to have Lucie
check it out. Barty and Anna Lea would probably
know who was parking it out there.

I decided to see them and hopefully get some
answers. The storm had started to gather earlier on
my way back to town. By the time I left the bank,
the wind had picked up and was blowing flurries of
snow. As I drove down their street, I could see the
Stacker house was dark, and there were no vehicles
in the driveway. I figured I could call Lucie Hansen
and bring her up to date, but I had nothing
meaningful I wanted to report yet. I needed to talk
to Barty and Anna Lea first. I decided to grab some
dinner, then come back and wait for their return.

It was dark when I drove back to the Stacker's
home. A dim glow showed through the front
window as I pulled up. I parked in front and walked
to the front door, which was slightly ajar. The sad
lament of some country singer filled the air as I
started to knock. Suddenly, I could hear Barty's
muffled voice.

"Come in. I've been expecting you."

I entered the small living room, which was so
dimly lit that I could just make out his form settled
in the big recliner on the far side of the room. He
looked rough, bleary-eyed, wearing a tattered
undershirt and sporting a three-day growth of beard.
He did not look prepared for a social visit. In his
hand was a tumbler of amber liquid, whose source,
a half-full twenty-six of Crown Royal, sat on the
table beside him. All of this was picked up in a
glance. What really caught my attention was the

rifle lying across his lap.

"Have a seat!"

He motioned me toward the sofa with the rifle.

"I was wondering how long it was gonna take you to put it together. My wife's old man phoned me that someone was nosing around the Chevy. When he described the stranger, I figgered it was you."

"I was told that was the car, which came out to the well when I wasn't there, so I wanted to find out who it belonged to."

Barty laughed as he waved the rifle around.

" It's mine. I park it there. Now you know. So what?"

I could see that Barty was drunk, but I had no idea how dangerous that made him. I felt continuing the conversation in his present state was probably not a good idea. I got up and started to leave.

"Sit down! You're not going anywhere."

Although the rifle was waving around, he managed to keep it pointed in my general direction. Feeling very unheroic, I sat down and waited him out.

Finally, he seemed to calm down a bit and went on, "I came out to see you cause we needed to talk, but you weren't there. I guess your buddies described my car, but that was okay cause I found this in your trailer."

Barty reached behind his back and produced a gun, which I recognized immediately as my Magnum.

"You should be more careful about leaving these things around in unlocked drawers. Dumb things like that sometimes come back to bite you in the ass. I'll bet you been wondering where this was."

I could feel my anger beginning to take hold; I was getting sick of listening to this jerk.

"So, what the hell good does that do you, sneaking in and stealing my gun? Does that make you feel like a big man?"

"Hmmm," he smiled. "We're getting to that, but don't you want to know what we needed to talk about?"

"Barty, I don't give a damn about you or what you wanted to talk about."

"Oh, but I think you will. It was all about your precious Elena."

I almost felt the physical jolt when he mentioned her name. Up to that point, I had essentially no suspicions that any of this related to her.

"I was going to warn you to stay away from her."

I remembered I had somewhat sensed in the bar that night that Barty was a bit protective of her, but not to this extent.

"Why? Did you think I was going to hurt her?"

"God, you're stupid. You don't get it, do you? I was in love with her, and I was pretty sure she cared about me. I knew that some day we would be together. I just had to get her to feel as strongly about me as I did about her. I did everything to show her how I felt. I fixed the trailer up real nice for her and helped her in any way I could. When Charlie Baker tried to date her, I told her he had a whole bunch of kids up on the Reserve. Where Tom was concerned, I had to make up stories about him to make her lose interest. And then you came along, and she got serious about you real quick. The only thing I could see to do was get rid of you."

"So it was you that shot at me last month."

"Yeah, I don't know how I could have missed. I don't hardly ever miss with this thing," he said with pride as he cradled the rifle.

"Why are you telling me all this? Just go down and tell the cops and solve all our problems."

"You really, really, really are stupid," he screamed. "You're not going anywhere, ever, so just shut up and let me finish."

At that point, I knew Barty was going to shoot me, and I had to figure out a way to take him down or talk him out of it if I planned to see another sunrise.

"So, I come home from work. The old lady was off somewhere with the kids. If I'm gonna eat, I'm gonna have to fix it myself. I see the light on over in the trailer, so I go over to see Elena. She's all excited and invites me in to tell me you two are going to get married. It was a shock. I couldn't let it happen. She knew how I felt about her. I begged her to go away with me instead."

Barty's eyes were starting to glaze over. He had been sipping continuously on the whiskey as he talked and had slipped lower in the chair with the rifle resting on his knees.

"I told her how much I loved her and needed her," he sobbed, "but she just looked at me as if I was dirt."

Now was the time. I started up off the sofa but never took a step. Barty was faster than I figured. I felt the searing pain in my side, as I saw and heard him fire the rifle. The impact drove me back onto the sofa. I sat clutching my side, as the blood started welling out between my fingers.

"It's your own damn fault," he yelled. "I warned you. Do you really think I'm going to let you walk out of here? I've got it all worked out.

You're gonna die after you try to kill me with your own gun."

He reached down beside the end table and came up with my Magnum. He pointed it over his shoulder and fired two shots into the wall behind him.

"Didn't know you were such a bad shot, did you? Couldn't even hit me from over there. The police are going to find it in your dead hand, the same gun that shot your girlfriend. My little trip to your trailer paid off well."

Barty was sobering up fast with the adrenaline pumping through his body.

"I'll save you the details of what happened. Let's just say I had to have her my way, and I wasn't going to let her go running back to you afterward."

He raised the rifle again and fired a shot into my shoulder. My arm went numb, and I could no longer control the bleeding in my side. He raised the rifle again. I closed my eyes and waited for the finishing shot. When the gun went off, it sounded different, and I wasn't hit. The first thing I saw when I opened my eyes was Barty in the chair with a mass of blood and entrails, where his lap used to be. The terror in his eyes was directed behind me. Anna Lea was standing in the doorway with a shotgun. Calmly she pumped another shell into the chamber, walked over to her husband, and blew away most of his face with the second shot. She dropped the gun and collapsed on the floor.

Somehow I pulled myself to the phone at the other end of the sofa. I dialed 'O' and managed to tell the operator to send help before I passed out.

20

I could hear the sound of a stream in the distance, the babbling of water running over gravel. It was very soothing. I wanted to open my eyes to see it, as my mind was picturing a brook running through a quiet meadow, but the effort was too great, so I relaxed and just enjoyed the sound. As it got progressively louder, it mysteriously transformed itself into human voices, very close and not as pleasant to hear.

I dragged myself up from my comfort zone to see three uniformed hospital attendants gathered around my bed.

"You finally decided to join us," someone said. "We weren't too sure for a while."

My mind was identifying the words, but since they weren't making any sense, I closed my eyes and tried to recapture the image and sounds of the brook.

When I awoke again, it was nighttime. The door to my room was closed, but enough light sneaked in to illuminate my situation. A myriad of tubes and wires were attached to my body, which made for a very discouraging first vision. I was about as awake as I was going to get and felt lousy, probably due to all the stuff that appeared to be pumping into my veins.

I tried to piece together the last events I could remember. Foremost was the image of Barty's shattered body sprawled out in his chair, and Anna Lea crumpled at his feet. The events of the evening slowly filtered back through my mental haze, which was beginning to dissipate with the morning light. This new awareness also brought the discovery of my arm, shoulder, and the upper half of my torso immovable in a cast, the onset of pain, and a nurse by my bedside. She was a matronly lady of middle age. Her name tag spelled out 'Emma.'

"How are we this morning?" She asked chattily.

"I don't know about you, Emma, but I feel like crap."

"I think we can do something about that, but you're going to have to deal with a certain amount of pain. We can't justify pushing much more morphine into your veins. If you've got questions, you can get your answers from the doctor. He'll be in around ten."

"Just two questions."

"Go ahead."

"What day is it?"

"Monday."

"That can't be right. It was Monday evening when I got shot."

"That's right. You've been out of it for almost a week. What's your other question?"

"Where am I?"

"Saskatoon City Hospital."

The doctor showed up around noon. He sauntered casually into the room and sat down on the end of my bed.

He was a small man in his fifties, slim to the point of skinny. His salt and pepper crewcut bristled like an unwashed brush, matching a carelessly trimmed mustache. He had the sunken cheeks of someone who had lost too much weight too quickly or simply had forgotten to replace his dentures that morning. Most noticeable was a pair of piercing blue eyes, which appeared to be totally aware of his surroundings. He was dressed in the traditional Lab coat, which didn't quite hide a vivid blue tie, stained with some unidentifiable portion of his breakfast. His accent gave him away as either a Brit or an Aussie.

"Good morning. I'm Dr. James Gordon. Welcome to the world. I must say you had us going for a while to keep you in it."

"How bad?"

"Well, the good news is that you are in much better shape than the bloke who attacked you. You lost a lot of blood, almost bled out before the paramedics got to you. They gave you a transfusion and rushed you down here. Putting your shoulder back together was a surgical adventure, but with the help of pins and wire, we, fortunately, had very few pieces left over. Since we added stuff, we figured we should balance it by taking something out, so we took your spleen, or what was left of it. The bullet tore it apart after taking a little chunk out of your stomach. You're lucky he wasn't using hollow points, or we wouldn't be having this conversation."

"Don't I need a spleen to keep on living?"

"Well, you don't have one, and you're still alive. You'd be surprised how many people are walking around without one. It just acts as a filter for the blood, like a filter in your car that cleans the petrol before it reaches the motor. Your immune system will be a little weaker, and infections may be more difficult to treat, but you'll survive. With your apparent lifestyle, I'm sure something else will get you before the lack of a spleen becomes an issue. Besides, I spent too much time with you on the operating table to let you cash in."

I was just getting back to sleep after an exciting lunch of soup and jello when Lucie Hansen walked in.

She stared at me for a couple of minutes with that tough cop look of hers until I started to laugh. Then she softened.

"I'm still really pissed at you. I thought you'd gone back home. Why couldn't you have kept in touch and let me know what you were doing?"

"Because it wouldn't have made any more sense to you than it did to me at the time, and besides, you still had me figured as a suspect."

"That's probably true," she replied. "So, tell me the whole story of what happened. I need to record it on tape for my report, so try to remember every detail, if you can."

I took her through the whole chain of events from my meeting with Lonnie in the bar to checking out the Suburban at Anna Lea's parent's home and finally to the point of passing out in the Stacker living room.

Lucie turned off the machine and said, "You know, at one time in all of this, I did consider Barty Stacker as a suspect but didn't think him capable of something like that. You never know about some people. As for your account of the evening, I took a statement from Mrs. Stacker, and her description of the last half hour is almost identical."

"Why do you find that a surprise? She was

there."

"Because of the kind of shape she's in, I'm surprised she remembers anything."

"How is she?"

"That's what they're trying to find out in the Psych Ward. We need to get their report to decide if we're going to lay charges against her."

"Why the hell would you charge her? She saved my life."

"I know," Lucie replied. "That holds for the first shot, but neither of you was in danger after that. Yet, according to you, she calmly walked over and blew her husband's head away with the second."

"Forget the word 'calmly.' She was walking like a zombie. As far as I'm concerned, she was not in the real world when she took that second shot."

Lucie thought for a minute then replied, "If this goes to trial, would you be willing to testify to that?"

"Absolutely."

"Okay, I'll come back in a few days and keep you current. You need to concentrate on getting healthy."

For the next ten days, I focused on getting my body healed. Doc Gordon came in one morning and proceeded to cut away the cast. This was followed by a painful manipulation of my arm and shoulder.

"It looks like I'm going to have to get you up on the operating table again."

"How come?" I asked with concern.

"Oh, it has been a slow week, and I need something to do. But seriously, there is just too much tightness and too little range of movement. I need to make a few adjustments for you to have maximum use in the future."

He did the shoulder rebuild the next morning. The procedure went well, and the new cast was lighter and much easier to deal with.

Another week and I was antsy to go home.

As promised, Lucie Hansen showed up again. She was out of uniform for the first time since our trip to LaRonge, and she looked good. A well-tailored suit hid her tendency to plumpness. Her hair was styled, and carefully applied makeup enhanced her natural beauty.

"Wow, did you get all dolled up just to visit me?"

She blushed but replied. "Not completely, I have another non-police related meeting this afternoon. I've taken your advice and decided to look at some opportunities to set up my own investigation business when my retirement day comes."

"That's great, Lucie, stay with it. Now tell me what has happened with Anna Lea?"

"The Attorney General's office decided not to lay charges against Mrs. Stacker. The shrinks reported her as temporarily insane at the time but say she is okay now. They could see no further reason to hold her."

"You still sound dubious."

"I am. It just doesn't fit. I've interviewed her twice now. Either she's on the level, or she is a hell of an actress, and right now, I'm not sure which."

"What about her kids?"

"They're with her parents, and that's the other thing. She doesn't seem particularly concerned about taking them home."

"I can understand that. That's where all this went down. Those kids are old enough to understand what happened. Why take them back there to live?"

"Sure, but right now, she's living in the house without the kids."

The next morning, when Doc Gordon came in, I tried to get a handle on when I would be released.

"So, you're getting tired of our company already, are you?"

"I am. You folks get too much joy out of inflicting pain."

He chuckled.

"How about another ten days. Beds around here aren't in short supply for a change, so we can keep you long enough to get the cast off and see if the shoulder is responding the way it should. If so, you're out of here."

This proved to be the case. My shoulder appeared to be healing faster than expected. My release was scheduled for two days. My big regret was they didn't release me that afternoon, in which case I wouldn't have undergone all the emotional turmoil and heartache that followed.

The next day, just after lunch, an attractive woman came into my room. She was of average height, with long honey-blonde hair tied back in a ponytail. Her body was slim but well developed in the right places, highlighted by a form-fitting sweater. A tight wool skirt ending mid-thigh accentuated her shapely legs. She walked over to me, bent down and gave me a long passionate kiss on the lips.

"I've been wanting to do that ever since we met."

Up close, I recognized Anna Lea but not the Anna Lea Stacker I had known. Gone was the mousy little wife of Barty Stacker. The replacement was a shocking but definite improvement. The constant sadness I had observed in her eyes was gone. In its place was a look of; I don't know what to call it, sort of a mixture of mystery, joy, and instability.

"I loved the shocked look on your face. You didn't recognize me, did you?"

I agreed I hadn't and thanked her for saving my life.

"Actually, you helped me save mine. I had been slowly dying for years until that night."

"What are you telling me, Anna Lea?"

"I'm telling you the hassle you got into with Barty allowed me to do something I've wanted to do for years, kill that son of a bitch."

That stopped me.

"You mean you planned it?"

"Hell, no. I just took advantage of an opportunity. When I returned home, I heard the first shot as I pulled the car into the driveway. I had no idea what was happening. My first thought was that a burglar had gotten into it with Barty. I grabbed the shotgun he kept in the garage, came in and found him getting ready to shoot you again, so I fired, somehow knowing I wouldn't go to jail for saving your life."

"Okay, but what about the second shot?"

"That one was for me."

"Why?"

"Ever since we were first married and even before, Barty ran around on me, screwing other women and treating me like crap. If I complained, he beat me up. I put up with all of it because of the kids, but Elena was the final straw."

The door in my mind was slowly opening, and Shelly was telling me not to ask the next question, which sprang to my lips.

"What do you mean?"

She looked at me, and her face became a kaleidoscope of emotion.

"I once vowed to myself I would never tell you this, but now I think you need to know. Elena and Barty were lovers from the first day she moved into the trailer. Almost every day until you arrived, he would spend most of the evening with her. After she hooked up with you, she wasn't his any longer. I could see it was driving him crazy, and I took a lot of pleasure in watching him suffer. I had the feeling he was going to snap, and something was going to happen, and that I should warn you, but I guess I thought you wouldn't believe me."

So, there it was. The door to the little room in my mind was wide open now, and the words of my father came tumbling out again. They had been locked up for so long this time. I remembered they tried to get out when I first met Elena, but I wouldn't let them. I didn't want any doubt about her.

Anna Lea sat silently beside me and then asked, "What are you going to do?"

"Go home and try to sort all this out."

"Are you going to tell that woman cop what I've told you?"

"Look, Anna Lea, you saved my life. The why or other circumstances are irrelevant in comparison. I owe you, and I'm not going to repay you by telling your story to the police."

There were tears in her eyes as she took my hand.

"Will you come and see me if you're ever back this way?"

"I will, but I hope I never see Amyot again."

"I know," she replied, "I'm going to gather up

the kids and move down here and start my life over. I don't ever want to see that town again, either."

She put her arms around me, kissed me again, and left.

I only saw her once more a few years later in Saskatoon, where she had a good job and was happily remarried.

The next day Kellie flew up in her Dad's Cessna to take me home. She brought Jeremy along to drive my truck back. Once we got him on his way, I settled down in the seat next to her as she got clearance to take off. Finding a comfortable position for my shoulder in the small plane was no easy matter. When we were up, and on course, Kellie turned to me and said, "We're three hours out of Calgary, just enough time for me to hear your whole story. Things sure went to hell after I left. Guess I should have stayed and looked after you."

Although I was getting tired of going over the whole sequence of events, I figured I owed it to Kellie, so I told it once more. Initially, I had decided to keep the details of Anna Lea's visit to myself until I had it sorted out in my mind, but that hadn't worked so far. I had come to trust Kellie's instincts regarding people, so I related that last conversation to her.

She listened in silence and said nothing for a few minutes.

Finally, I asked her, "What should I believe, that Elena loved me as she professed, or that she was Barty's mistress and was just using me to get out of Amyot?"

Kellie thought for a moment longer then said, "I sense to some extent you can believe both. I knew Elena well enough to be fairly sure she truly cared for you. I can't see she was using you. In fact,

I think it was Barty she was using before you arrived. I understand that. On occasions, I've used sex as a tool to get what I wanted, with no feelings of remorse. It was that way with Danny at first. I needed some excitement to counter the boredom of the wellsite, and Danny was more than happy to provide it. Anna Lea was probably telling you the truth. I can see no reason for her to make it all up unless she was hot for you and wanted to dirty your memory of Elena. It does sound like she had feelings for you. I can't comment on that, as I never met her. I can accept the idea that Elena was probably using her body to get a good rental deal and other benefits until you came along, and she fell in love. Dusty, you had her built up in your mind as a saint, when in reality; she was just another flesh and blood woman with all the desires and weaknesses of our sex."

"What you are saying should make me feel better, but it doesn't. My mind can't accept both explanations. You are probably right about having her on a pedestal, but isn't that what happens when you fall for someone?"

"Sure," she replied, "for a while until you get to know each other. Then you start seeing their flaws and weaknesses and the things about them, which begin to bug you. You just didn't know each other long enough to reach that stage."

It was strange as I listened to her. I began to feel like I was a teenager again, and Shelly was telling me about life and love

21

Spring faded into summer as I struggled through my recuperation. The advice from friends that time would ease the pain of Elena's loss was given with good intent. Unfortunately, it wasn't working. So much time spent by myself only intensified the sadness. It was made worse by the fact I still didn't know what explanation to accept. I knew what I wanted to believe, and most of the time, I was able to convince myself that Anna Lea had made the whole thing up. But then the doubt crept in, and I ended up back where I started. I finally realized I probably would never know for sure, so I should put the whole thing behind me and get on with my life. Time was spent getting my strength and flexibility back as well as turning down jobs I was physically unable to undertake, and those I had no desire to do. Among the latter was an offer from Martin Angleton to manage his new exploration and development company, Amyot Resources. I still wasn't ready to become a suit, and I sure as hell didn't want to go back to Amyot. Unfortunately, Jeremy came under Kellie's spell and took their offer to abandon the classroom for the boardroom.

Marty Kalloch took me out for lunch a couple of weeks after I returned.

"When can you go back to work?"

Without waiting for an answer, he went on, "My client wants to put big bucks into the Foster Lake claims, and he wants you to run the program. I explained to him about your situation and told him you probably wouldn't be able to take it on right away. That doesn't seem to be a problem. I figure if we can get the induced polarization and electromagnetic surveys done this fall or late summer, we can probably postpone the drilling program until winter. The question is, are you up for it?"

My first thought was to turn down another Saskatchewan job. My second thought was that it was a better offer than anything else available.

"Sure, I should be able to deal with it about mid-August."

"Great. I'll sign up a good crew to help you out."

"What about Reuben? Did he ever show up?"

"He did. He arrived at his daughter's place about a month ago. Rollie phoned me about the same time looking for work and told me he was back. It seems he went cross-country to Pelican Narrows to visit his brother after he left your camp. He took sick on the way and almost didn't make it. They nursed him back to health."

"What about those claims Rollie was trying to peddle?"

"Reuben staked them down at the southwest end of Lower Foster, well out of our area of interest. He did it before you got up there. Evidently he was following up on a tip from some guy in the bar."

"Well, I guess that explains a few things. Are you interested in them?"

"I don't know. The gold assays are interesting. I'm going to check the ground out on my next trip up there."

"By the way, Rollie said your friend, the lady cop, was up in LaRonge and talked to Reuben about the two missing prospectors. When she left, Rollie figured she was satisfied Reuben had nothing to do with their disappearance."

I told Marty about my trip with Lucie to Jenny Lake, obviously leaving out the more personal details.

Marty thought for a few minutes then said, "I wonder what they were onto. Normal people don't go to all that trouble to stake claims without a valid reason."

"Two problems with that, based on what happened, I don't think we are talking about normal people, and secondly, there is very little outcrop in that area. It's mostly swamp."

"I know, but I think we should have a look."

By August, I was getting anxious to do something and more than ready to get out of the city. Marty agreed to have everything set up and ready to go by the fifteenth. I decided to go in early and do a bit of fishing and prospecting. On a whim, I phoned Lucie Hansen to tell her I would be passing through Saskatoon and to see if she could spring loose from her busy schedule for a cup of coffee.

Lucie agreed and said she was about to phone me as she had some updates. I assumed they had to do with Reuben, finally making an appearance and being absolved of any part in the disappearance of the prospectors. I couldn't have been more wrong.

I arrived in Saskatoon in the middle of the after-work gridlock. It was pouring rain, and traffic was a total snarl. I phoned Lucie, and she gave me directions to her place. She was just getting off work and said she would meet me there. I arrived just as she was pulling into her parking spot behind a modern fourplex. She greeted me with a hug and invited me into her ground floor suite.

"You certainly look better than the last time I saw you," she observed.

"And so do you," I lied.

She had lost at least twenty pounds, her face was drawn and haggard and the sparkle was gone from her eyes.

"No, I don't. I look like hell. Dusty, I'm just totally stressed out from overwork and an important relationship that ended badly. Life has not been good for the past few months. I need a vacation to go somewhere and not think about anything except eating, drinking, and lying in the sun."

"Don't you get some holidays so that you can get away from it?"

"I do, but I don't seem to be able to get out of my rut and go."

"Well, I'm going back up north for another stint near Lower Foster, but the job doesn't start for another week or so. In the meantime, I'm flying up to McTavish Lake for some fishing and prospecting. There's a small cabin, a sand beach, and the water should be warm enough for swimming. You're welcome to join me, get away from it all, and do your own thing. There are no ulterior motives or hidden agendas on my part. It's up to you."

"Are you sure you're not trying to get me back in that sleeping bag?"

I took her question seriously until she started to laugh.

"I thought about it, but figured I'd never be able to recreate that scenario."

Lucie declined my offer to take her out for dinner. Instead, she opened a couple of cans and we had a simple spaghetti meal.

Afterward, as she was tidying up, I brought some dry wood in from her porch and got a fire going in the fireplace.

"I guess your news is that Reuben Delaveaux finally showed up."

"No, I figured you'd hear about that through your northern grapevine. This is something else. It has to do with the events, which happened at Amyot."

She paused for a couple of beats, looking at me with a strange expression. Then she went on, "I've argued with myself for the past couple of weeks whether even to tell you this, but your call yesterday triggered my decision. After the last time I saw you, you were released from the hospital and had returned to Calgary. By then, the Stacker's house had sold. Anna Lea had already moved out with the kids and left it with her father to sell. The buyers didn't want the trailer left there, especially with the history behind it, so the Branyons, the next-door neighbors, agreed to have it hauled over to their property. They decided to renovate and clean it up for their daughter and her husband to live in."

Lucie went over to the large walnut desk, which occupied a corner of the living room, opened a bottom drawer, and pulled out a leather-bound book.

"They found this book behind a panel in the kitchen. It is Elena's diary, which she kept for the past year or so, with entries up to the day she was killed. I've read through it, and it is disturbing. I've thought about it, and I'm still not sure whether you should read it."

I guess Lucie expected me to get quite agitated and seemed surprised at my calmness, but I could see where all the mental turmoil I had been suffering since Anna Lea's visit might finally be resolved.

"Lucie, don't worry. I probably know most of what is in there. Anna Lea visited me in the hospital and told me that Elena and Barty had been lovers until I arrived. It was a shock, and up until the last few minutes, I have refused to let myself believe it was true. Without actually telling me, you have confirmed it. I appreciate your concern for my feelings."

She sat down next to me on the sofa and took both my hands in hers. The concern was still in her eyes.

"Dusty, that's not all of it. Elena and Barty Stacker were doing it right up to the day before she died. It didn't stop when she hooked up with you, and she was pregnant."

The last statement took my breath away, and I could sense that any trace of feelings left for Elena was rapidly eroding.

"When did she know?"

"Here, let me see," she said as she thumbed through the diary. "She indicated that she suspected it in mid-November, but wasn't sure until she went to see the doctor in Meadow Lake later on."

I was without words or feelings for a long time. Finally, I said, "So, she was pregnant before we ever made love, and accepted my proposal of marriage after her pregnancy was confirmed. Anna

Lea probably knew this but didn't tell it all to spare me. "

"Who knows with her? You know I've always been puzzled about that second shot she took at her husband. Now I think all of this probably explains it."

I started to pass on my feelings about Anna Lea's actions but stopped as I realize I would be jeopardizing the future of this lady who had saved my life. Instead, I replied, "I don't know, Lucie, the way I remember that night, she was pretty screwed up and not acting rationally."

"You've said that before, and I sense you believe it, but Dusty, are you sure you're not still trying to protect her? I can understand if you are."

"What difference does it make? You decided not to lay charges last spring. How has it changed now, except that you can perceive a motive? I'm not that versed on how things go in court, but I still don't think you have enough to make it fly."

She thought for a minute then said, "You're probably right, and I guess you wouldn't volunteer to testify for us if we tried."

"That's about it," I replied.

Lucie picked up the diary and handed it to me. It was a strange sensation, holding a portion of the story of the life of a woman I had loved but hardly knew. I turned it over in my hands, feeling the smoothness of the leather covers. I closed my eyes, pressed it to my forehead and unleashed Shelly's voice from the silence in my mind. He was telling me to let it go like he should have so many years ago. I didn't need or want to know the details. I just wanted to let it go.

"I don't want to read it, nor do I want to have it."

"What should I do with it, Dusty? Should I send it to her parents?"

"No, I don't think we want to destroy the good memories they have of her."

We sat together without speaking until I observed, "The fire is getting low. I'll get some more of those logs."

"I have a better idea," she said as she dropped the diary into the brightest part of the blaze.

We sat together on the sofa without speaking. Everything was coming together in my mind. I finally realized that Shelly's fixation on true love and most of the advice he gave to his son was wrong. It was mostly his way of rationalizing his own messed-up life. Based on his fatherly guidance, I had been searching for that person who would be my one true love, when, in reality, I should have been cultivating the friendships I had found. I took Lucie's hand and thanked her for all she had done in helping me work through it.

Rather than shut me out in the rain to find a motel for the night, Lucie made up a bed for me on her sofa. After she had retired, I sat up, trying to put it all together. Shelly had so much believed in love, and it was his eventual undoing. It had taught him not to confuse lust with love. And now his son, apparently having learned nothing from his experience, had made the same mistake. But maybe they are not mistakes and are just the natural progressions of human emotional development. To Shelly, initially, the love for my mother was everything. She was never a best friend. And so it was with Elena. I loved her but never knew her as a friend. She didn't live long enough, and if she had, we would probably have drifted apart or remained together in a loveless prison of marriage. Maybe, with Lucie, I had finally found a friend.

Still, disregarding the most important piece of my late father's advice almost cost me my life and will probably haunt me for the rest of my days.

GLOSSARY

Aeromagnetic; maps, surveys: A magnetism measuring device (magnetometer) inside an aircraft, or towed behind records magnetic fluctuations produced by the underlying rocks. These values are plotted on maps, and contours of equal magnetic intensity are drawn.

Anomaly: A value or set of values that deviates from the normal.

Assay: The result of a chemical test on a mineralized sample to determine its metal content.

Basement rocks: In a well-drilling context, the basement rocks, the Precambrian, below which no sedimentary rocks occur.

Blazes, blazed line, blazed claim line: When mineral claims are staked, the line running between the initial and final posts is generally identified by slices of the outer wood chopped from the trees along the line.

Bottom-hole sample: When a zone of interest is penetrated, a sample of the cuttings from the bottom of the hole is circulated to the surface.

Cache; food cache: Camp supplies are often hidden or located above ground to be inaccessible to animals.

Cap a well: A successful well that is scheduled for production at some future date is capped until that time.

Catwalk: A platform extending out some distance just below the rig floor for laying down core barrels, testing tools, etc.

Cement plug: A portion of cement placed at some point in the wellbore to seal it.

Chert: A very fine-grained, hard, dense sedimentary rock with a high quartz content.

Chopper: A helicopter.

Circulating; mud, sample: Pumping drilling mud down inside and up outside drillpipe to condition hole and bring drill cuttings to the surface.

Claim; staking, posts, tags: Mineral claims staked as defined by a blazed line with posts at both ends with inscribed information and metal tags fastened to the posts.

Claim block: An area larger than a single claim defined by a blazed line and posts.

Cook tent: Temporary building in camp where meals are cooked and served.

Conservation Board (Government): Provincial government division in charge of drilling records and samples.

Core, coring, core barrel: Coring is the process of cutting a continuous cylinder or core of the penetrated rock. The core feeds into the core barrel, which is attached to the bottom of the drill pipe. A special diamond bit is used for coring.

Derrick; derrickman: The derrick is the upper structure of the drill rig. When the drill pipe is out of the hole, the stands of pipe are stacked in the derrick. The derrickman works from a platform (monkey board) part way up the derrick when pulling pipe out of the hole or running back in.

Disseminated: Refers to minerals that are dispersed throughout a rock rather than concentrated in one area.

Doghouse: Covered enclosure adjacent to rig floor where records, orders, and geolograph are kept and a place for workers to get temporary relief from the cold.

Drill; drilling: A well is created by penetrating the earth with a drilling rig that rotates a <u>drill string</u> with a bit attached to create a hole 5 to 50 inches in. in diameter.

Drill pipe; drill string: This is the connected collection of the drill pipe, drill collars, tools, and drill bit. The drill string is hollow so that drilling fluid can be pumped down through it and circulated back up the void between the drill string and the casing or open hole.

Drillers: The person in charge of the drilling operation. Drillers generally work eight or twelve hour shifts.

Drilling break: When the penetration per foot rate speeds up.

Drill cuttings; samples: Rock chips, produced by the bit that are circulated to the surface by the drilling fluid.

Drilling mud; drilling fluid: A mixture of chemicals in water or oil designed to provide the correct characteristics to safely drill the well. This includes cooling the bit, lifting rock cuttings to the surface, preventing breakdown of the rock in the wellbore walls and overcoming the pressure of fluids inside the rock.

Drillstem test; test tool: A drill stem test (DST) is a procedure for isolating and testing the pressure, permeability , and productive capacity of a geological formation during the drilling of a <u>well</u>. The test tool is connected into the drill string at a point opposite the formation to be tested. It is sealed off from the rest of the hole by packers and then opened by rotating the drill string to allow fluids or gas to enter.

Drill time Recorder; geolograph: Records the rate of penetration

Dry hole: A hole drilled without encountering economic amounts of oil or gas.

Electromagnetic survey; map: This is a procedure that measures the electrical conductivity of the subsurface rocks. Contour maps are prepared from the recorded data.

Electric logging: Running an electronic tool in a borehole to measure electrical, radioactive, and sonic characteristics of the rock strata.

Engineer: Representative of the oil/gas company responsible for hole conditions, testing, logging, etc.

Environmentalist: A person who wishes to protect the quality of the natural environment by minimizing or prohibiting harmful human activities.

Formation: A rock sequence identified as being different by nature of how it was created, age, or distinguishing rock types.

Gas detector: A device that measures any gas entering the drilling fluid and sets off an alarm.

Gas kick: An alarm set off by the gas detector when gas enters the drilling fluid.

Gas plant: Natural-gas processing plants purify raw natural gas by removing common contaminates such as water, carbon dioxide (CO_2), and hydrogen sulfide (H_2S).

Geologist: On the wellsite, the geologist is concerned with the rock strata being penetrated, processing the drill cuttings, and identifying any porous hydrocarbon-bearing zones.

Geolograph, drill time recorder: Records the rate of penetration.

Geophysics: geophysicist: The study of the physics of the earth and its environment.

Granite: An igneous rock formed within the earth's crust from cooling magma and contains crystals of quartz, feldspar and ferromagnesian minerals.

Granite wash: A sedimentary rock composed of granite sand formed by erosion, generally lying on top of a granite basement.

High pressure zone: A porous and permeable zone containing gas under higher than normal pressure.

Hole conditioning: Drilling mud is circulated in the hole to clean out rock fragments and drill cuttings prior to coring, electric logging, drillstem testing, and running casing.

Horizon: A rock strata, formation, or zone.

Hydrocarbons: Oil and/or natural gas.

Induced polarization survey: A geophysical technique used to identify subsurface materials, such as ore minerals. An electric current is induced into the subsurface through two electrodes, and voltage is monitored through two other electrodes.

IP: Initial post of a mineral claim.

Jars: A mechanical device included on the drill string to deliver an impact load to stuck pipe generally in conjunction with a drillstem test.

Lag time: The time it takes a circulating mud column to bring a drill cutting to the surface.

Lease; lease road: Area of the wellsite and access road, which are leased from the land owner.

Limestone: A sedimentary rock formed by the accumulation of shell fragments from marine animals or by precipitation of calcium carbonate.

Limestone reef; reefal limestone: Fossilized coral reef.

Logging: Determination of electrical, radioactive, and lithologic properties of a rock sequence.

Lost circulation: Occurs when the circulating drilling fluid disappears into a very porous formation.

Mapping: Plotting geological or geophysical characteristics of the underlying rocks over a defined surface area.

Mineral deposit: Above average concentration of economic minerals.

Mineral rights: The rights to all minerals underlying a defined surface area. The rights may be owned or leased.

Monkey board: The platform, part way up the derrick, where the derrickman handles pipe.

Mounties: Members of the Royal Canadian Mounted Police.

Muskeg: Northern swamp

Oilpatch: A term used to include all aspects of the oil business.

Oil stain: Drill cuttings and cores from oil-bearing zones will show stain.

Oil fluorescence: Crude oil fluoresces in a range of colors, from dull-brown through to bright-yellowish and bluish-white. This phenomenon is used in drilling to identify very small amounts of oil in drill cuttings and core samples.

Outcrop: Bedrock exposed at the surface.

Packer: A device that can be run into a wellbore as part of the drill string when running a drillstem test. It has a smaller initial outside diameter that then expands externally to seal the wellbore and isolate the zone being tested.

Perforate: To create holes in the production casing to achieve efficient communication between the reservoir and the wellbore.

Permeability: permeable rock: The ability, or measurement of a rock's ability, to transmit fluid.

Pinnacle reefs: A conical fossilized reef, higher than it is wide, usually composed of limestone, in which hydrocarbons might be trapped.

Porosity: The percentage of pore volume or void space, or that volume within rock that can contain fluids.

Production: casing, string, pipe: Casing that is run for a successful well that is to be put into production.

Production tests: Tests run on a completed well to determine such factors as rate of flow, pressure drawdown, etc.

Precambrian Shield: The oldest igneous rock zone, which acts as basement and is exposed as bedrock over much of Northern Canada.

Radioactive area: An area that shows higher than normal gamma-ray readings.

Retaining harness: Allows derrickman to safely lean out from work platform to reach drill pipe in the center of derrick or mast.

.**Reservoir:** An oil or gas-bearing zone capable of production.

Rock magnetism; magnetic survey: Rock magnetism is the study of the magnetic properties of rocks, sediments , and soils. Surveys can be carried out from aircraft or on the ground.

Roughneck: Rig worker with lowest status.

Rig; drilling rig: A drilling rig is a machine which creates holes in the ground. Drilling rigs can be massive structures housing equipment used to drill water wells, oil wells, or natural gas extraction wells. The term "rig," therefore generally refers to the complex of equipment that is used to penetrate the surface of the Earth's crust.

SAIT: Southern Alberta Institute of Technology

Sandstone: A sedimentary rock composed of sand grains cemented together.

Satellite camp: A smaller camp situated some distance from a main camp.

Samples: Pieces of drill cuttings carried to the surface by the drilling mud and collected at the shale shaker.

Sample vials: Small clear plastic containers for storing washed representative samples at predetermined intervals.

Sample catcher: A roughneck with the task of collecting samples at regular intervals, washing them and delivering them to the geologist.

Schlumberger: A major well logging company.

Scintillometer: A Geiger counter with the ability to differentiate as to the source of the radioactivity.

Scrubber: A device used to extract sulphur compounds from natural gas.

Sediments: Solid fragments of inorganic or organic material that come from the weathering of rock and are carried and deposited by wind, water, or ice.

Sedimentary rocks: Sedimentary rocks are formed by the deposition and cementing of sediments on the earth's surface and within bodies of water.

Shaker screen: A wire-cloth screen, which vibrates while the drilling fluid flows on top of it. The liquid phase of the mud and solids smaller than the wire mesh pass through the screen, while larger solids are retained on the screen and eventually fall off the back of the device.

Shale shaker: This is a component of drilling equipment. It is used to remove cuttings from the drilling fluid.

Siltstone: A sedimentary rock with cemented silt grains, smaller than sand.

Silver nitrate test: A chemical test used to determine if a core contains salt water. The soluble silver nitrate combines with the soluble sodium chloride in salt water to form the insoluble silver chloride, which appears as a white powder.

Spudding: The initial penetration of a drill in the ground

Staking: Defining the boundaries of a mineral claim by means of claim posts and blazed lines.

Staking rush: Many people coming into an area to stake claims once a mineral discovery has been reported

Stand of pipe: May be one, two, or three joints of pipe together as a unit, depending on the size of the drilling rig

Stratum; strata: A stratum is a layer of sedimentary rock or soil with characteristics that distinguish it from other layers.

Surface hole; casing, pipe: The surface hole is drilled down through the overburden to bedrock. Large diameter casing is run and cemented shutting the hole off from groundwater or other contaminants.

Tar sands: A sandstone in which oil has been trapped; the lighter compounds evaporate, leaving a residue of asphalt in the rock pores

Tight hole: A well that the operator requires be kept as secret as possible, especially with regard to the geologic information

Tool pusher: The location supervisor for the drilling contractor. The toolpusher is usually a senior, experienced individual who has worked his way up through the ranks of the drilling crew positions.

Topolite thread: A biodegradable thread used by claim stakers and surveyors to measure lines. The thread unrolls from a spool which shows the number of feet or meters traveled.

Traps: An arrangement of rocks suitable for containing hydrocarbons and sealed by a relatively impermeable formation through which hydrocarbons will not migrate.

Vein: A distinct sheet-like body of crystallized minerals within a rock.

Weight material: A high-specific gravity and finely divided solid material, usually barite, used to increase density of a drilling fluid to counteract high-pressure zones.

Wellhead: The surface termination of a successful well that incorporates equipment to provide pressure control of the well in preparation for the production phase.

Wellsite: The location where a well is being drilled.

Wellsite trailer; shack: Living quarters for personnel (geologist, engineer, toolpusher) who are on twenty-four hour call.

Also by Guy Allen

<u>Bush Camp</u>
An adventure novel with a
Northern British Columbia mining
exploration camp setting

<u>Talisman</u>
A historical adventure set in the
goldfields of California in the 1850s

<u>Sun City</u>
Murder, mining scams and dope
runners in sunny Arizona

<u>Huntress</u>
A young woman's search for her
kidnapped family in 1850's California

Previews and first chapters of all
books can be viewed at
http://www.guyallen.ca

Paperback and Kindle EBook Editions
Available at Amazon.com

Guy Allen is a retired geological engineer with many years experience in mineral and in oil and gas exploration in North America. He and his wife Geri live in New Westminster, British Columbia

Manufactured by Amazon.ca
Bolton, ON

11903829R00146